THE WHITFIELD RANCHER BOOK 2

KATHI S. BARTON

This is a work of fiction. Names, characters, places, and incidents are products of the author's imagination or are used fictitiously and are not to be construed as real. Any resemblance to actual events, locations, organizations, or persons, living or dead, is entirely coincidental.

World Castle Publishing, LLC
Pensacola, Florida
Copyright © Kathi S. Barton 2017
Paperback ISBN: 9781629897912
eBook ISBN: 9781629897929
First Edition World Castle Publishing, LLC, September 4, 2017
http://www.worldcastlepublishing.com

Cover: Karen Fuller
Editor: Maxine Bringenberg

Chapter 1

Dylan didn't like this one bit. Rules, she understood those, except the fact that there was no bending of them, even in situations like this one when she felt that her way was the right way. Nor could she fly by the ass of her pants. Rules, she kept telling herself, were a good thing. Of course, she thought that killing the man would have served them all better, but then again, that wouldn't help. It would be good though, just not helpful. But that didn't mean she couldn't make the fucker pay, and pay well for his stupidity. Stretching her neck again, she let out a long breath so she'd have control, or at least the appearance of it.

"You say that you had to steal from the leap because it was your right as a member. And that it mattered little to you that there is a system set up that allows you to have food so long as you let someone know what you're doing?" The man in front of her nodded and smiled at her. "Wipe that grin off your face right now, jackass, or I'll do it for you. Permanently."

Evan cleared his throat but said nothing. He was, like he

had a dozen times already, reminding her that she needed to be a leader and not kill them all. Stupid rule, that one. She supposed it made sense. If she killed all the idiots, she'd not have a leap to lead. That thought did have some merit, but she didn't think others would see it her way. Again, the fucking rules.

"I was hungry. And since, as the leap leader, you're to provide for us, I took what I needed." There was a flaw there, and she wasn't sure why anyone else hadn't picked up on it. "I'll be taking a bit more too, the next time I go by it."

"Well, things will suck for you, I guess. I've taken care that it's all safe and sound." He just grinned. Choosing to ignore it, she moved on. "Anyway, what do you do for a living? I mean, other than take food you didn't purchase for yourself, and basically steal from the hand that helps you."

"I don't have a job at the moment. I'm between them." He laughed, and so did the four men with him. Men she had to deal with too. "Is this going to take much longer? I have some shit I have to do. And of course, I gotta get me something good to eat."

"The leap larder is empty, as of nine last night. Also, there is a signup sheet for those that need something from it, and rules regarding it." The man—she forgot his name because she'd been calling him dickweed—objected. "I really don't care what you think is unfair, you idiot. I'm in charge of this, not you. Also, as of this morning by approval from the council, every able-bodied member of this leap will work. Whether at an outside job, meaning not leap work, or something for the leap. What is it you're good at, besides stealing and being a lazy fuck?"

"I don't want to work. It interferes with my nap times."

The men with him laughed again when he turned to look at them. Dylan looked at Evan who shrugged. She was on her last bit of patience with this group, and he knew it. "Besides, it's your duty to provide for those who don't have anything, like housing and food. And if I can't afford my bills for power and the like, you're supposed to pay those too. You can do it. All rich and mighty Whitfields like you could."

"Yes, it is my job. Or I can cut you loose. That's one of the rules too. One I like, so you know. You did read that one too when you were looking for loopholes, right? If I can't pick and choose the ones I want to use or not, you can't either." He stared at her, mean, like he was going to hurt her if her words didn't suit him. Dylan stood up and let him see that she was armed. "You can be pissy all you want, you little fuck. As of right now, you have ten days to get your shit together and get out, or you find you a job that you work at for forty a week. Or I can find you something suitable. And trust me, you don't want that to happen."

"You're not being very nice to me, Dylan. I thought for sure, being a woman and all, you'd be more sympathetic for me." He grabbed his crotch and shook it, like that was something sexy. When Evan stood up, she moved to the man and grabbed his cock hard. "Christ, lady. That's too rough. You like it that way?"

Putting pressure on his dick made her feel better, and when he whimpered she smiled at him. Squeezing on his little twig and berries more, she watched him pale. It was going her way or he'd be dead. Evan was well within his rights as her mate to kill him. She knew that.

"This is how it's going to work. Are you listening to me?" He didn't answer, so she squeezed harder and he begged her to stop. "So, are you listening to me?"

"Yes. Christ, yes, I'm listening." She told him again what was going to happen. "I don't want to work. Fuck, bitch, you're going to pay."

She let him go and moved back when he puked on the ground in front of her. He looked up at her, his eyes full of hate. When he opened his mouth, she kicked him in the head. He was out before she put her foot back on the ground. Turning to the other idiots that had fucked up her day, she asked who was next.

Each of the other men dropped to the ground and rolled to their backs. She had read about this in one of the books Evan had given her. Something about exposing their most vulnerable part to her. But she wasn't entirely sure why they were doing it to her. Turning to Evan, he smiled and gave her a thumbs up. Well, if he said it was okay, she would go on.

"This is how it's going to work with the rest of you. Either straighten your asses up or you'll be gone before you can say shit. Understand?" They each said they understood and called her master. "A job has been found for each of you. You work it, you'll get help when you need it. Otherwise, you'll be gone, just as dickweed here is going to be when he wakes up."

"Mistress?" She told the man on the end to stand up. "He's got a mate and a couple of kids. You gonna kill them? If so, well then, I can't be here no more. She and them kids, they didn't do nothing to you but be his mate."

"I'll look into that. And I'm not a monster. I'm just a leap leader that wants everyone to be treated fairly, and dickweed here wasn't allowing that. I give what I get in circumstances like this. It's up to you guys if you want to stay or not, but I won't put up with bullshit. Not one bit of it." He nodded and she released them. As they slunk off, she turned to Evan when he sat by her. "They're going to fuck up, you know that, don't you?"

"Yes, but not for a week or so yet. Are you kicking him out? His name is Jared, by the way, not dickweed." She snorted. "Right. Anyway, I have to go into town. My last time this week, I promise. Then I'll be off call and we can have some fun."

"We have fun a lot now, dork." He took her hand in his as they made their way back to the house. "It's almost done, isn't it? I mean, we only have the yard to finish up and then it'll be complete."

"Yes, and that can't be worked on entirely until the spring. Adam is waiting to see what comes up, whether it's all weeds or some flowers too. Are you all right? You've seemed sort of off all morning. Are you still bothered about what the counsel did?" She looked up at him as he continued speaking. "They made the right choice, baby. You're very good at this, and things have already improved in the few weeks you've been doing it."

"Yeah, well, if they let me do it my way, I'd have it whipped into shape already." He laughed. "I'm only joking. But it does seem to be going so slow."

"You'll get it turned around, I know it. In the meantime, we have that meeting with David on the book. Then the dinner with Mom, Dad, and Grandda. By the way, making him your second counsel was fantastic. He's loving every minute of it." She told him he was teaching her a lot too. "He'd be the one to do that. I've never seen him so excited. Thank you for that."

"It was really for selfish reasons. I miss my own grandda more than I thought I would, and Ollie is a good man. Funny, and he doesn't cringe every time I open my mouth." She laughed. "I love your mom, but I tell you, she's a prude. Every time I mention sex or cuss, she gets all kinds of red in the face. To tell the truth, sometimes I just do it to hear her fuss at me."

"I think she's figured that out too. Just the other day she asked me the meaning of a couple of those words. And let me tell you, I don't know which of us was more embarrassed, her or me. So from now on, when you do that, make sure it's something I'm not going to have to explain to her later." Dylan laughed. "Or I can make you tell her. I think that would be better."

"No thanks. You think she gets red when you talk to her? I'm sure that if I have to explain them to her, she's going to flare up like a flame. No, she's better for it with you." Dylan thought of a couple more words she could use around the elder Whitfield, and decided to add them to her vocabulary the next time they were together.

After Evan left for town, she sat down at her desk. The sucker was bigger than their bed and filled with more electronic equipment than their kitchen. Not that she ventured in there much, but she did get a glass of tea and hurry out at times. The room gave her the willies.

The phone on her desk rang at lunch time, and she answered without looking. There was only one person that used it—the president—and he wanted her to do something. She loved when he called; it meant she could have something to do rather than just clean-up work in the yard.

~~~

Sunny moved through the crowded restaurant with only one thought in mind…a glass of tea. Her tea maker had died a few hundred miles back, and she'd not had the chance to get another one. And the guy that came by and had saved her life, whoever he was, had done enough for her, and she didn't want him finding her another one. Besides, she was pretty sure that he'd stopped coming by.

He'd left her drugs when she was first hurt. As well as changed her bandage when she wasn't able to. Sunny didn't know who he was or why he was doing it, but she was grateful to him. She had no idea where she'd be if he hadn't, other than six feet underground.

When she was able to order, she told the guy what she wanted. The man behind the counter didn't bat an eye when she asked for the largest tea he had. He simply turned around, pulled a gallon of the nectar from the icebox beneath the counter, and put it in front of her. The urge to pick it up and drain it made her mouth water. Paying for the tea, she made her way back to the camper.

She pulled a glass from the cabinet and poured some while standing there. If it was as good as it looked, she'd get another one. Otherwise this one, like the others she'd gotten in the last two hours, would be dumped only to try another place. Thankfully, it was as delicious as she'd ever been able to make herself, and she enjoyed a second glass while thinking about her life so far.

She had figured out who she was by the newspaper article that she'd found on the countertop a few days after waking up in this thing. The paper had run an article about how she was missing, along with a picture of her. Things started to fall into place after that. Not everything, but enough to know that she owned the camper, and she'd been able to piece together some of what had happened. She'd been shot. By who, she didn't know yet, but it was for something that she was working on. What that was remained fuzzy, but she was alive now so she could find this person and take care of whatever had happened. Or so she hoped.

Sunny, or Sunshine Davis, was an investigative reporter. Freelance, and apparently pretty well known. People everywhere were looking for her. Not all good, she supposed, not with her being shot up, but she was well thought of in some places. She also knew that she had a sister and brother who were looking for her.

"Not that I'm reaching out to them." That much had been a revelation too, that while she had family, they hated her. Funny, she thought, she didn't like them either. "Money grubbing shits."

Standing up to make her way to the icebox—not fridge, but an actual icebox—she put the tea inside it and made room for more. Since she'd cleared out most of the food in it a few weeks back, she'd not done much to replenish it. Not that she couldn't, but with travelling, things tended to get too warm, and she wasn't up to being sick on top of everything else. Tonight she was staying at a campground, and then tomorrow she was going to find this leap.

There wasn't anyone to ask about them. She'd looked them up on the computer that she'd unearthed a few weeks ago. There was a lot there if you cared, but she'd not found that much personal information. They were wealthy, that much was obvious, but there wasn't a lot on them really, until recently. The fact that it was a large article about one of them getting a new home and how lavish it was made her think that either these people were a big deal or it was a slow news day, maybe both.

Getting around was much easier than it had been even a

couple of days ago. Today she hadn't taken any of the pain medication that had been left for her. And she could eat a little better. Things, to her at least, were looking up.

She glanced at the closet where her personal items had been stored. She had money, a great deal of it. Not that there wasn't some in her bank accounts, but the closet was filled with the green stuff. Sunny was sort of afraid to count it, fearing it would be more than her head had thought. And that was a large number.

It's not that she had lost her memory about the money. With the exception of the last few minutes before she'd been shot and a few days after, she remembered it all. But the money had never been there, not that much anyway.

Sipping her tea, she decided to try and have a little dinner. Sunny hadn't ever been a big eater, but lately she'd been having consuming more than her usual salad and crackers with cheese. Yesterday she'd eaten three hot dogs and french fries, plus a malted milk.

The man appeared before her just as she stood. Reaching for a gun that wasn't on her, she braced herself. Sitting down, she waited to see what he wanted. It was the one from before, a tall very slender man in dark clothing. Sunny was sure that he was a vampire, and if not, something similar. Not that she'd ask him, but she was curious.

"Vampire. My name is Tanner. I don't remember now if it's my first or last, but it's all I go by nowadays." He asked if he could have a seat, and when she nodded he did so, but he was very prim about it. "I'm here this time. The last few times, I've only been here in shadows. I think you remember that. I have the ability to come and go as I please as well. But that is neither here nor there. I have a few things to tell you.

You're not going to be thrilled about a few…the rest, well, I suppose we shall see."

"All right. But I've figured out a few things. Mostly, if you mean that you've given me your blood, I'm okay with that." He thanked her. "Why me? I mean, not that I'm not thrilled shitless that you saved my life, but why?"

"The man that shot you—and killed you, by the way—was someone that I know. I cannot tell you anything about him until you remember. That's the rule." She nodded. "Why you? Much more complicated than you might wish to be a part of."

"Doubtful I'd turn you down. As I said, you saved my life." She watched him get up and make a sandwich for her. It was thick with roast beef, tomatoes, and other things she knew were not in there this morning. "You fixed that from what stuff?"

"I should have thought about the icebox and it not working when you were traveling. I don't have any use for such a thing, nor does my staff. I have taken care of that now. This no longer requires ice to keep it cold, and it will stay this way for you. It is cold and stocked. And will be until you reach the Whitfield ranch. You must go there." She asked him why. "There is a man there—his name is Oliver, but he goes by Ollie—an older gentleman that can help you. You'll need it with this man coming for you. And he will…you've ruined his business with your exposé. Do you remember him?"

"Alfred James. He's been doing some testing on animals for a long time, and usually just paid the fine, but I found out that he was testing on some humans, ones that didn't sign on to his sort of work." Tanner nodded. "He also had a few disposal issues that came up when I was doing my research.

Mostly with the bodies of the people that he used."

"Yes. And had you had this uncanny power that you seem to have developed lately, you would have known that few of them were actually human." She was afraid of that power, but didn't say anything to him. "You should use it more, Sunshine. Should you do that then you'll get better at it. I must admit, I was startled by it, but after looking into a few things, I've concluded that it was a combination of your death, my blood, and the drugs that you were taking. Again, that is part of what I needed to tell you."

She could touch things. Well, duh, she thought to herself. Everyone could, she supposed. But when she did, freaky things happened. Stories came to her. She could not just see the person that had held it, but their life history too. Not all, but enough to know how the person was feeling when they had it. The vampire had been her first, and she was sure she knew things about him that no one else did.

Finishing the sandwich, she regarded the man in front of her. He looked to be only in his mid to late thirties, but she knew he had to be much older. He dressed well, but not overly lavish. He was educated, highly so, and was also street smart. She liked him. And for whatever reason, trusted him.

"This thing that I can do, I've figured out that no matter what it is, if I touch it for long enough, I can read, or whatever it is I do, all about it. Like the last owner. Names, addresses, as well as tell if they're dead or not. Kind of creepy, but in my line of work, it could also be very useful."

"Yes, I would say so. But back to Ollie. He is a good man, one you can trust with your life. He has some...let's just call them connections to the paranormal world that will keep you hidden away until you're at full strength. His oldest grandson took a mate, and she has become a leap leader that you will need as well. Very strong as well as mouthy. Much like you." Sunny smiled. "I don't know if you realize this, but that wasn't a compliment."

"Sure it was. Being mouthy is what keeps me around. I mean, other than bullets, I can worm my way out of most anything." He laughed when she did. "And this man, Ollie, he will help me hide out, then what?"

"You'll be able to do your research for me. Alfred has another plant, one that I've not been able to find. My hope is that he has this other lab, and there is where you'll find my family. My kiss. But most importantly, my mate." She nodded and asked how many were in it. "My kiss is of about twenty vampires varying in age. One of them being my mate, as I said."

"She's still alive then?" Tanner said that he was, as far as he knew. "I'm sorry. Yes, then. He. Can't you connect with him or something? I don't know a great deal about how that will work. But you connect with me, correct?"

"I cannot connect with him because he's somewhere that is blocked from me. I know him to be alive because I have not felt his death. And I would, as I would yours should you meet with another killer. He is still alive, but for how long, I know not." She nodded as she began to take notes. "I will help you as much as I can, but I cannot show myself as easily as you would be able to. You'll be safe, as safe as they can make you, with the Whitfields. Ollie, he is aware that you're coming."

"What sort of cats are they?" He told her and Sunny looked at him as a chill washed over her. "I don't like tigers. I knew one once."

"Yes, I know." He didn't say anything else but watched

her. "Ollie is a good man. And his family are the best people you'd ever want to meet."

"If you say so."

She sat there long after he was gone, but wasn't sure about this now. Tigers? She was more than a little terrified of the fuckers.

Once, when she'd been working in a warehouse to find out what sort of shit they had going on, there had been a couple of them, big fuckers that roamed the place when it was in lockdown. The larger of the two had played with her for a while before he pounced. She'd spent three hours with him letting her go then chasing her down to cut her up again. Sunny had never been so glad to see the police as she was that next morning. Then she was off to the hospital to get several hundred wounds stitched closed, as well as her broken arm set. Those fuckers were a nasty group.

Not only had she gotten a great story on the crap that they'd been doing, but the story about the illegal use and poor care of the tigers had gotten her praise. If she'd been honest with the newspaper, she would have asked for a gun to blow the things out of existence. She hated them that much.

Chapter 2

David was sitting at his computer, reading the last entry that he'd made toward his book, when he realized that he wasn't alone. Looking up, he saw his grandda, and it appeared that he'd been sitting there for some time. Not waking him, he read a little more then shut down his computer after saving his work. Grandda woke about two minutes later.

No one he knew woke like his grandda…clearheaded and smiling. His face wasn't puffy, nor did his eyes look like he'd been asleep. Grandda was as fresh as a daisy after a spring rain, and was just as happy after a small snooze. David was both in awe and jealous of that feat.

"Sorry. I was up until late last night talking to an old friend, and I am more than a little tired today." David told him it was fine, he'd been working so hard that he'd not noticed him there. "Not a good thing, I don't think. Not with stuff…I have to talk to you about something."

"All right. I'm finished for the day. Would you like to go and get some dinner with me?" He said that he'd rather pick something up and come back to his house. "That's fine with me. I have some leftovers from dinner yesterday, potato salad and stuff, if you want to get some sandwiches to go with it. Mom made it all, so you know as well as I do that it's wonderful."

"Sounds good to me." David nodded and pulled on his jacket. Whatever was bothering the old man, he wasn't spilling anything right now. "What do you know of vampires?"

"I have a buddy that is one. He's not too old, younger than you, I think." Grandda asked if he thought he was old. "No, just using you as a reference. Why so touchy?"

"I don't know. I'm old, I know that, and I'm not getting any younger either. Dagburnit boy, when can I have a great grandkid?" David told him that he'd not been able to reproduce for some time now. "Smart ass. I should tell your momma."

"She knows I can't have them either. And in the event you're wondering, none of us grandsons can have them. At least not without the intervention of some major work and a female." Grandda laughed. "Okay, what do you want? Subs, burgers, or a real dinner?"

"I've changed my mind. Dinner. But we can't talk until we get someplace private. I mean it boy, don't be asking me about it, not until we're at your house." He promised that he wouldn't. "How about that place out on Maple Avenue? You know, the steak place."

When they were seated, Grandda asked him again about his knowledge of vampires. He told him what he knew, which really wasn't that much. Grandda said he'd tell him more when they were home. The dinner conversation was good, nothing too mind-tasking, and they were headed to his house in less than an hour.

Almost as if a switch had been turned, Grandda started talking. "About fifty or so years ago, I met this man. His name was Tanner. He didn't have a last name, and I don't think he's adopted one now. Anyway, he came to see me last night." David handed his grandda some iced tea as he continued. "He has a problem, and there is a damsel involved. He wants me to keep her safe."

Damsel? His grandda was forever saying things like that. Just yesterday he'd heard him refer to one of the waitresses at the ice cream parlor as a car hopper. He'd known what it meant, but he cautioned him on using it where she might hear him.

"All right. What's she done, or been done to her, that would require him, a vampire, to ask you, a tiger, to care for her?" Grandda pulled an old newspaper out of his jacket pocket and handed it to him. David glanced over it before laying it down. "She's a writer, for some pretty serious papers."

"Yes. She's one of them ones that goes in and finds things out then puts it all to paper. Not just that paper, but a whole lot of them. Freelance, I think he said she's called. She's good too, and honest, he told me. Just recently, within the last month or so, someone took exception to her articles and shot her." Grandda leaned back. "Tanner said he needs her. She is going to help him find out where his own mate has gone. He thinks he's still alive and at a part of this place that this girl was investigating. They shot her up enough that she was dead for a bit, but with his magic he was able to bring her back. She has an ability to touch things and find information about them now. We gotta keep that under wraps so no one else comes along and decides she might be more useful to them dead than walking around knowing stuff."

"I don't understand. Why doesn't he just give her something that belonged to his mate and have her find out where he is?" David was glad that his grandda wasn't too squeamish about the male to male mates. His parents weren't either when it came to sexual orientation. "I'm assuming that they've tried that."

"No, I don't think so. She's been hurting pretty badly, I guess, and he hadn't gotten around to it. But he doesn't think it'll work anyway. Not only does he not have many of his mate's things—they seemed to disappear when his mate did—but he's being blocked somehow, and that would mean, he thinks, that she would have the same issues. He's gonna try tonight when he rises." David asked why this woman. "I don't know if you want the truth of it, but I owe this man and I intend to see to it that she's safe."

He wanted to ask him why he owed an old vampire, but was pretty sure that he'd not tell him. Or worse yet, David might not want to know. His grandparents had been hellions back in the day, and if someone asked for details on that life, no one would ask again. A vampire in their list of friends wasn't a surprise, but that Grandda somehow owed him was. But David would not ask. Ever.

"Why is she unsafe? I can see where her looking into things would piss someone off, but to kill her? I'm not sure. What has she done?" He told him she'd found out some nasty stuff about Alfred James. "The guy who owns that drug company? I thought they were out of business. I mean.... Ah. So, she's the reason that he had to close his doors. Found out about the tests he was doing on some of the homeless."

"You heard about that? With your head stuck in that

computer of yours? Well, that's good. I was sure you'd been shut off from the world around you." David laughed when Grandda did. He had been spending a lot of time on his books. "When is your next one coming out?"

"You going to read it?" Grandda said he was not. "Yeah, I didn't think you would, which is fine. Two months. And this one I'm doing now, it's due out in six months. So, my deadline isn't that close, but I want to work on it all the time. But back to this woman…she's hurt Alfred and his business. That's not too far from here, I believe. You think he'd come here for her?"

"He has already." Well, he supposed that Tanner would know. "Tanner said that the man wants her dead. The fact that she's made it this far without him hurting her again is probably due to him thinking she's already six feet under. When it comes out that she's not, he's gonna come for her."

David wondered why she'd need to be exposed. "She has to write the paper, doesn't she?" Grandda nodded. "And he's sending her here because of this friendship he has with you, and he knows that you'll keep her safe. For her to do this other favor for him. Not that I know this man, but did he only save her because of what she can do for him?"

"I suppose so. Not that it matters, I guess. What's done is done, right?" Grandda got up to pace. He didn't say anything more, but he was thinking hard. David would help him, if for no other reason than he loved and respected the man, and he'd asked him to help.

"I'd think that staying low would be a smarter move, don't you?" Grandda said that he was never one to lay low. "No, I guess you're not. But this woman, she's already had an attempt on her life. I'd think she'd want to be quiet for the rest of her life."

"You'd no more do that than I would." Which was true, but he was a tiger, not a human, and told Grandda that. "I'm thinking that she's like Dylan. Damn the torpedoes and full sail ahead. But she's coming in a big camper. The kind that you drive around. Can she store it in your barn? And maybe hang out here in one of your bedrooms while I find her someplace else to live?"

"Sure. I mean, I'm not using the barn at the moment. And don't foresee any issues with her staying here. Like you said, it's a big house." David leaned back on his couch and thought about her living here. "Will Mom and Dad know why she's here? I don't want them thinking the wrong thing."

"Yes, I'll tell them. And you don't have to worry about the rest of them either. I'll make them see this is a good thing." David nodded, but said nothing. His family rarely did things the way he thought they would. "You're a good boy for doing this for me, David. I'll remember it."

He would too, remember the favor that he'd done for him, but David didn't care if he ever made it even. He loved the old man and was glad that he was there to ask it of him. When Grandda left, after telling him that Tanner would be around to see him when this girl got closer, he went back to his book.

David was having a good time with it. The research was getting easier, and he wasn't having any trouble with his publisher. Sometimes, with deadlines looming, she would hound him to death. This one, while she wasn't thrilled about the genre, she was giving him a good deal of time to get it done.

He'd already approved the cover for it, and she was

spreading it around with the blurb that he'd given her. The cover was a picture of the old house, before it had been renovated the first time. A woman was sitting in an antique rocker in the yard with a great many people around her, mostly blacks. She had been a person that helped a lot of the slaves in her time, which was what had made him want to write the history on the house. And it was rich with it.

The house, the same one that his brother lived in now, was finished. It had taken them a couple of months of hard work to get it good enough for them to live in. Now all that was left to do was the gardens, which was going to be a spring project to see what was there, and the barn being put in. The one there now wasn't so much a barn as it was a center for Dylan's other job…working for the president on covert operations.

David waited up as late as he could, but went to bed around two in the morning. He supposed that the man had gotten tied up and wasn't able to reach him. Yawning twice, he was almost asleep when his head hit the pillow.

~~~

Sunny parked in the space she'd been given. The park wasn't all that busy…just last minute campers getting in a couple more nights before it was too cold. Her camper was made for cold or hot weather, so she didn't have much to worry about, but checked things out when she was set up.

The camp host—Charlie, he told her to call him—said that the Whitfield ranch was about six miles out of town. She thanked him, and then he told her that old man Whitfield came in to have breakfast on Tuesday mornings at the restaurant in town. Since she didn't really know the day of the week, she thanked him again.

Now she knew it was Monday. Tomorrow she'd go and

25

talk to the man, hopeful that it was the one she needed to talk to, and get this done. She wasn't too keen on spending even one more night in the camper, if she was honest with herself. Three weeks on the road, and her recovery, had made her yearn for a real bed and a little more company than herself for a while.

The knock at her door about dusk had her pulling her gun. She'd had it on her all her adult life, knowing that there were a lot of lowlifes out there. Looking out the little peephole, she saw a driver's license shoved up against it, and saw the name Whitfield. Opening the door but not putting her gun away, she looked at him.

He was handsome in an elderly, rugged sort of way. She knew him to be cat, or so she'd been told, but the color of his eyes threw her. They were as blue as the skies in summer. He smiled at her, and while charming, she didn't trust him any more than she had an idea he thought she might.

"You're Sunshine Davis. Tanner sent me out here to talk to you. He's the vamp that told you to come here." Sunny made sure that he could see her gun. "Got me a granddaughter-in-law that carries one of them too. She's never pointed it at me, but I'm careful not to make her want to either. I'd like to talk to you, if you have the time."

"He told me that you'd know something about me that no one else does." Mr. Whitfield nodded and looked around before pulling out a little notebook. Tanner had mentioned that too, that the man's memory was a little fuzzy at times nowadays. "Your first name is Oliver."

"That's right, but I go by Ollie. My son, he prefers Oliver. I begged him not to name any of his boys that, and he didn't. Sorry name, Oliver. People always want to have you begging for food." He grinned at her. "You have a tattoo on your left ankle. It's a butterfly that is green and yellow. You got it on your eighteenth birthday. You also have several bullet hole scars that are healing nicely, and you have this ability to touch something and know all about it. Good enough?"

She let him in and the camper seemed so much smaller with him in it. She'd not noticed his bulk until then. When he was seated at her table, she sat across from him.

"I only paid for tonight. I was told that you have breakfast in town on Tuesdays. If you don't want people to be able to hurt you when you least expect it, then you should really change things up a little. No set schedule will be safer for you. If you need it." He thanked her. "Why you, Mr. Whitfield? I mean, there were any number of places that I could have hidden away for a while that was closer to my home."

"Maybe, like me, they have your set schedule." She told him that wasn't possible. "Wasn't it? You're good, but I'm betting that whoever is coming for you, he knows more about you than you think he does. My Dylan, she's Evan's wife, she could teach us both a thing or two, I'm betting."

"I was sent here to be safe and to help out your friend. Since he's...I can do some things that I couldn't before." He said that he'd been told. "Okay. Then I guess you understand that if someone found out about this creepy shit, I'd be in more trouble than I am right now."

"I'd say that's about right. But you don't have to worry none. I got you." She smiled at him and he grinned back. "I know what you're thinking. I'm an old man and can't do much in the way of helping a pretty little thing like you. Well, I got me a beast along with my family. And my granddaughter, Dylan, she's got her a bunch more that can be called upon to help us."

"She's the leap leader, I heard." The man's chest puffed out and he smiled. That was something she'd never seen anyone display...pride in something she'd done. "I'm not going to go into hiding and not publish this story. The paper that got him shut down, they didn't have all of it. There is a great deal more to this picture."

"I'm sure there is. And no one wants you to not do what you're good at. I, for one, hate that the man is still walking about like he didn't do anything wrong. But that's not my department, to take him down. You'll do fine by him." She hoped so. "Okay. Now, I have a grandson that is gonna help us out. He's got him a lot of house and no one sharing it with him at the moment. He and I talked, and he'll allow you to plant this rig of yours in his barn and stay in his house until we can get a few things figured out. Like how safe you are for now, and a place you can be in permanently."

By the time the old man had left her, she had an address, a burner phone as well as contact numbers, and the time she was to go to the other house. In the middle of the night seemed sort of over-the-top, but she said she'd do what he wanted. At midnight she was in bed. It had been a long few days.

Chapter 3

David put his paperwork away, along with the few items he'd been given to use as a reference. The book was the most helpful. There were other things as well, some mementos that he was going to have pictures taken of to put in the book. He wrapped the Bible up and put it back in the safe. Not that he thought anyone would steal it, but he wanted to preserve it as much as he could.

The noise outside had him checking his clock. "Right on time." He moved through the house toward the back door. His grandda was being very cloak and dagger about this whole thing, and he was having fun himself. Looking around the rooms as he made his way to the kitchen, he was glad that he'd had someone come in and clean up after him. The place hadn't been dirty, but there was dust everywhere, as well as papers. He wasn't a slob, but when he was into a book his research would take him all over the house. Smiling as he opened the door, he wondered what his new houseguest would think of him.

The camper was big. And while not new, he could see that it was well taken care of. The woman at the front of the thing waved at him, but she moved toward the back rather than getting out of the door near her. He figured she was going to be getting her things, and he went to the door to help her. The bulletholes in the door startled him. And when she came out, he looked up at her.

"Are you all right?" She frowned and told him she'd been better. "Did someone shoot at you while you were coming here?"

Confusion covered her face and he pointed to the door. "Nah, that was there when I got this thing from my parents. They're not real. I think one of my sister's kids put them on here, and I've never been inclined to take them off. I think they actually superglued them onto it. I'm Sunshine Davis, but everyone calls me Sunny. You must be David."

"I am. Do you have things to take out of here? I can help you if you do. Grandda said that while you're on the mend, you're still hurting a little bit."

He put his foot on the step that moved out for him, and nearly fell back when the thing shifted under his feet. Grabbing for the first thing he could, Sunny's hand filled his and he knew they were going down. He didn't want to hurt her or for her to be hurt, so he shifted his body and took the brunt of the fall. In seconds he was under her, and she was nose to nose with him.

That was when her scent hit him.

Pushing her hair out of her face, he wondered if she'd gotten her name from the color. It was as bright yellow as the sun, and softer than anything he'd ever touched before. Carefully—he could feel the gun in the front of her pants—

30

he ran his hand down her back to her bottom. There it was filled with the firm flesh, and all he could think about was rolling over and taking her. Instead, he tried to make a little conversation.

"You're my mate." She only stared at him, and it was then that he remembered her wounds. "I hurt you. I'm so sorry."

"I need a minute." Her forehead touched his and David lay still. To move now would relieve some of the pressure on his cock, but it would also hurt her more. "Just so you know, I'm not looking to be anyone's mate. I'm sort of in a pickle, as your grandda called it, and taking on a mate would be very dangerous to us both."

"Yes, I can well imagine, but it's true nonetheless." She looked up at him. "I would love to roll you over, strip you down, and taste every inch of you, but I would imagine that you're hurting."

"And how do you suppose that is helping? Just be quiet and let me think beyond hurting right now." He moved then and felt her shiver in response. "Look, buddy. We've just met, like seconds ago. I am not going to jump into your bed and fuck the life out of you, just because you're cute and sexy. Now behave yourself while I try and get my feet under me."

"You think I'm sexy and cute? That's wonderful. Because I think you are too. Who named you Sunshine? They deserve a medal as far as I'm concerned." She growled low and he laughed. "You know, that was pretty good. But my tiger is much better at it. You let us have our way with you and we'll show you."

"Behave." She moved then and moaned. Not in pleasure but pain. He knew this because she paled just a little more before rolling to her back and not moving. "I hurt in places

31

that you cannot believe. Who knew a few bullets to the body could take so long to heal? And as they did, the sometimes pain is almost enough to take a person to their knees. Or lower."

"You become a cat with me and you'll heal much faster. Also, and many don't know this, the sex is incredible." She glared at him. "We don't have to move. Just wait until you feel like you can."

"Then what? Are you going to jump on top of me and make love to me? I don't want sex. I want a bed, a real one. A shower that has lots of hot water. A kitchen that doesn't require me to stand in one place and cook in shifts. I need a clean towel. Fluffy slippers, and a robe that isn't older than me." He moved the strand of hair from her cheek and told her they had all that and more. "Mr. Whitfield, you aren't pulling any crap on me. I've been around men like you for most of my life. You'd say whatever you thought the woman wanted to hear, then leave her broken and shattered on the side of the road. Please, just don't do this right now."

When she frowned, he watched her face. This time she was thinking, and hard. Touching his fingers to her cheek again, he watched her as she struggled to work whatever it was out. He was sure that she got it when she looked at him.

"The man that shot me. I know him. His name isn't there, but I know his face. He said that he was working for Alfred James." He waited, for some reason knowing that she worked things out verbally. "He didn't like me snooping around in his business. Said that he was there to tell me why he was shooting me and to kill me because of Alfred."

"Don't think of him, but his face. Tell me what he looks like." She closed her eyes and he had the most profound need to kiss her. "Just start with his eyes. What color are they?"

"This guy shot me, and you want me to tell you what color his eyes are?" He nodded at her when she looked at him. "You think this will help? Because, and I have no idea why, but I believe knowing this jerk would go a long way in finding him easier."

"Sometimes not thinking of something will help you think of it. Now, his eyes. What color are they?" She told him they were brown. "Okay, his hair. Straight? Curly? Bald?"

"His hair was grey, cut short like he's very particular about it. He has a scar on his forehead that he got from playing in a tree that he was not supposed to be in." David said nothing. That was a memory that he was sure she'd not realized that she had. "He has thin lips, so much so like he didn't have any. He grew a mustache to cover it up, but it did little good since he's so.... Christ."

When she sat up, he did as well. David didn't push. As much as he wanted to, he didn't try to get her to tell him who this prick was, because as surely as he was sitting there, the man was going to die. She turned to him and he watched her fall apart.

"My brother. He shot me. He…well, he killed me. I knew that he hated me, my sister does as well, but he actually had no trouble killing me." David stood up, helping her as gently as he could. He could smell the fresh blood on her. "I need some things out of there first. Then...I guess we need to talk."

"Yes, but not until you're ready. What's his name? Your brother and your sister too?" She told him she'd let him know when she got the things she'd need out of the camper. "All right. But I'm helping you. I can smell that you're hurt again, and I don't want you to be in pain."

While she gathered a few things, mostly clothing from the camper, she was quiet. It gave him the opportunity to contact Evan. He was a surgeon, but a doctor first. He knew he had awakened him the moment he asked him what was wrong.

I have a mate. The silence at the other end of the connection between them was funny. *The woman that Grandda told us was coming. She's hurt, as you know, but when she fell out of her camper, she landed hard. Can you come over and have a look at her? I know nothing of her gunshot wounds yet, but I also don't want her to be in pain.*

I'm coming now. David thanked him. *Dylan is as well. She wants to talk to her about who shot her.*

She remembered who it was. Her brother. Evan asked for his name. *She hasn't told me as yet. She's being very safe, I think. Why should she trust me already? Sunny is going to come into the house with me and talk. I figured that with you here helping her out, you'd hear it as well. Sunny said that he and her sister have hated her for a long time, just so you know.*

Evan said they were on their way and that Dylan was having the leap keep an eye on things for them. After thanking them, David helped her carry the things into the house. She was bleeding enough that it had soaked through her shirt, so he had her have a seat on the couch while he took her things to the spare bedroom. As much as he wanted her in his room, he didn't want to push his luck. The gun she had on her lap didn't make him feel very welcome right now.

Evan was in the living room with her when he came down the stairs. And Dylan was asking questions in her usual, not so gentle manner.

"What the fuck do you mean, you'll get around to it? I'm the sort of person that you don't want to fuck with. I don't

34

care who you are." Sunny stood up when Dylan did. "You don't scare me."

Sunny reached out to push Dylan back. It was something he might have done to one of his brothers had they been all up in his face. But the moment that her hand connected with the skin on Dylan's shoulder, both of them cried out as they were tossed away from each other. He rushed to Sunny just as Evan did to his mate.

"What the fuck was that?" Dylan sat up as she spoke, but didn't move. Not that it looked like Evan was going to let her. "You zapped me. What the fuck did you do that for?"

"I saw them. All your men. They're dead." No one moved as Sunny spoke softly. "They were there when you were killed. The fact that you're alive and they're not, it bothers you badly. They're gone and you're alive."

"Who the hell have you been talking to?" Sunny stood up with David's help, and he led her back to the couch. "That's the crazy shit you can do? What Ollie told us about? That's how you figured you know so much about me? Well, I got news for you, you don't know shit. And I'm all right."

"Of course you are. And I don't want to know shit about any of you, but it seems like I'm stuck here. Can someone please, for fuck's sake, give me something to knock me out? I've been banged around enough today."

Evan moved, but David stepped in front of him. He wasn't sure what he was going to do, but Evan wasn't going to hurt his mate.

"I'm going to give her something for the pain, then have a look at her wounds." David tried reasoning with his cat, but he wasn't having it. "Look at me, David. I'm not going to hurt her. Move, please, so that I can make her pain go away."

Moving, he sat down next to her. Taking her hand in his, he was glad that she didn't jerk away from him. He was having enough trouble as it was, holding his cat at bay. When he looked at Dylan, she was sitting down too and looked concerned. He asked her if she was all right.

"Yes. I'm sorry that I hurt her. While I knew about her ability, David, I didn't know that it would work on people." He nodded and glanced at Sunny. She was looking a little shellshocked herself. "Evan, see about her, okay?"

He let his brother look her over, and found that she wasn't hurt as badly as he'd thought. The blood was from a wound she'd gotten in the barn when they'd fallen. It didn't need any stitches, thankfully, but Evan did offer to wrap it up.

"However, if you let his cat clean it, it'll heal in a matter of seconds." David winked at Evan for that, then back at Sunny. "You should be as healthy as you can be, what with the shit you have going on around here."

"I know what you're doing. Trying to get him to bond with me. I have no wish to hurry things along in that department." Sunny looked at him, and he felt like he was a bug pinned to a wall. "You will behave. We've talked about this before."

"We have, yes, but I don't want to." Kissing her on the mouth, he moved away before she could retaliate. He was sure she was planning it, but for now he'd gotten more than he'd hoped for. "The camper is buttoned up, and I've called in a friend, Nate Briggs, who is going to have one of his men go over it to see if there are any bugs on it. Tanner said that he had already, but we want to make sure nothing got on it between then and now."

"Also, so you know, there are a number of leap around the property. Tigers for the most part, but also some wolves.

When you have a moment, you should let one or two of them sniff you, or have a little taste of your flesh, so that they can know your scent." He wasn't surprised by what Dylan said, but he was that Sunny agreed so readily. "And for my information, could you give me the names of your brother and sister and anything you might have on them that will help? I'm assuming that you don't want them to know where you are."

"No. I don't. My brother is Sam, Samuel Davis. He's my twin, and about an hour older than me. Madeline Richards, or Maddie to most people but her, is our older sister by about eighteen months. Our parents are gone. Died some years ago when they both were in a hotel that was swept away by a current in another country." Sunny got up to pace as she continued. "My sister is a horrible person, and Sam isn't all that much better. They'd both steal the pennies off a dead man's eyes and not think a thing about it. While they both have money, though not a lot, they somehow think that I should be giving them more. As in paying for their kids to go to camp. Supplies for the special classes they make them take, as well as any sports. To their way of thinking, since I have no children, I should be spending my money on theirs. I don't, but that's what they'll say when they find me."

"I see." Evan laughed a little before he spoke again. "And do they hurt you when asking, or is it more of an annoyance sort of thing? Either way, they're not going to touch you again, not while we're here."

"Nah, they don't hurt me. Or at least they haven't done it on their own. They've paid to have me hurt in the past, but they cut that shit out until recently. I've learned to fight back, and that usually costs them more when the other party needs to be patched up. I take a lot of pleasure out of making sure they have to be patched up a great deal." She began walking faster, taking harder steps. "I've just figured out from some memories coming back to me that Sam is the one that shot me. I know that he was working for Alfred, though at what capacity, I was never clear on. Not in an office setting, nor did he have a real title. Sam didn't know my part in bringing his boss down, at least I don't think he did, but he lost his job too when the company closed. He could be holding that against me, I suppose, but Sam shot and killed me. I was only dead for a few moments, according to Tanner, but long enough that I got this freaky touch thing."

"And this freaky touch thing, does anyone besides us and Tanner know about it?" Dylan looked at David when Sunny told her no. "If this gets out, even to one or two dicks, she's gonna be in deeper shit than she is now. Not just for her ability, but what else someone might think she can do. Like, can she talk to the dead? Does she know things about the dead that they don't want out there? People won't let that shit go, you know this."

"Yes, I know." He stood and picked up one of the few things that he'd not put away from the chest that Bailey Hutchinson had left to him when he died. "I'm not asking you to show off, but I would like to know the extent of what you can do. You touched Dylan and that gave you some insight on her, but what about this? What can you see on it?"

He knew that she didn't want to touch the small cup. It was part of the set that he'd unearthed when he'd been digging around in the sublevels of Evan's home. The rest of it, all twelve place settings, were being carefully cleaned and cataloged. Dylan had donated it to the women's circle that was going to be in charge of the historical center when the remodeling was finished.

There were other things as well. Books with handwritten notes in them. Curling irons that had to be heated on the stove. Handstitched linens that were still as beautiful as they had been so long ago. And they'd found furniture too, some of it older than the house itself.

"What if I break it?" It was a good question, but he didn't think she would. He thought that the power that they both held, she and Dylan, was what had made the snap between them. "All right, but just so you know, I don't know what this will tell you. This is new to me as well. And though Tanner told me to practice to get used to it, I've avoided touching things for just that reason. It scares me."

"Anything that you can add to my research will be helpful. If it's nothing, then we're not out anything at all. But I just want to see how much you can tell us…that way we can gauge how strong you are." She nodded. "It'll be fine, Sunny. We're all here for you."

David

Chapter 4

Sam sat with his family and decided that they were not all that nice to be around. Not that they were cruel, nor were they loud, but they were boring. Just like the books he had in his study. Getting up before the movie started, he made his way to his private library to close the door and take a short nap. Anything to stem the boredom. No one, not even his wife, asked him where he was going.

He took out his keys and opened the drawer to the bottom of his desk. There was a false bottom there, and he pulled out the pictures that he'd put in there a month ago. Smiling at them, he laid them out over his desk in the correct order and stared at them, remembering the night he'd taken them. Christ, it had been the most fun he'd ever had, followed by the best sex he'd had in ages.

His sister was dead, and he'd done it. The money had gone a long way to making up for all the shit he'd been into of late, but having her dead was a bigger thrill than he'd thought it would be. He picked up the first picture and leaned back in his seat to stare at it before going to the next ones.

The camera had been a part of the deal he'd made with Alfred. He'd had to wear the video recorder and let it record him killing Sunny. It had been easy for him to get a few copies of the stills he'd seen, and now he got his rocks off just looking at them. The night he'd killed her, he'd fucked his wife, Mary, so hard that he'd been sore the next day, and so had she. Christ, it had been spectacular.

The second picture was the still after he'd gut shot her. It had her on her knees with her body bent. There was blood too…not a great deal, but enough that he'd known she was as good as dead. And when he'd shot her again and again after that, he'd danced around her body for several minutes.

Sunny hadn't been a terrible person, not really. Yeah, she did bitch when he told her about bills she needed to pay. It was stuff for his kids, never him or Mary. She had it…Sam knew she made good money taking people down. And since she had no children or a husband, she could certainly pay for his and Maddie's kids to have some fun. It wasn't as if he signed them up for things they didn't want to do. But damn it, lately she'd been telling them she wasn't going to pay anymore. That had pissed him off.

Shooting her had been fun. The fact that he'd gotten to see her die before leaving had made him giddy. Taking the pictures of her, then later showing them to Maddie, had made him feel like a gangster. But then…. Sam frowned when he thought of when he'd been ready to leave her there.

Her body had simply disappeared. The blood was still there, as well as the outline of her body in it. But she, her gun, wallet, and even her shoe that had fallen off, were all gone.

It had scared him at first. He'd thought her some sort

of otherworldly creature that had turned to ash or air when she'd been died. But she hadn't been inhuman. He knew that because she didn't come after him. And had she been inhuman, then he would have been as well. They were, after all, twins. But something had either taken her dead body or something else had happened.

Not that he knew what else it could have been that had taken her away. He had looked at the recording several times before turning it over to Alfred like he was supposed to. And Sam was relieved that the older man hadn't mentioned it. He'd been so happy that Sunny was dead that he'd not cared where her body was. Other than to ask if she'd been taken care of.

"She has been. I don't want that coming back to bite me in the ass either." Of course, Alfred had no idea that Sam had made a copy of the recording for himself; that little bit about her disappearing was only for his knowledge. "It was easier than I thought it would be. She wasn't nearly as smart as she let on."

"Yes, well, she did get in and out of my plant without either of us knowing she was there."

Actually, Sam had known, but not until she'd gathered enough to get them all in the dog house with the government. Sam had given the tip that Alfred received to let him know he might be in trouble. He wished now that he'd let him know his name, but there was time for that later. Sunny was dead, and now he was going to be able to collect on a lot of things. Like her insurance. Insurance that he was reasonably sure Maddie didn't know about.

He knew Sunny had some on herself. When he'd been snooping around her house after she'd been gone for a few days last fall, he'd found the policies. He wasn't the beneficiary in them, of course. She didn't like him, after all, nor their sister, Maddie.

Sunny was giving the money to some kind of hospital that cared for little kids when they were sick. Not that it wasn't a good cause, he supposed, but he was her only brother. And he should benefit from her death much faster than some stupid kids would. And he'd have fun. Which, if she liked him, she'd want him to with her money. It was crazy thinking, he knew, but then she was nuts anyway if she thought that he'd let that amount of money go to someplace other than his bank account.

Sam had looked into that kind of legal stuff. He was her blood relative, and he could have that shit taken care of after she was dead. The article he'd read had said it could be years before it would be overturned, but it wasn't like he needed it. It's just that he wanted it. And why not? He was as deserving as those kids were…more so, because he'd had to put up with her being related to him all those years.

Sunny hadn't been cooperating with Maddie or him for months now. When he'd sent her the notice about his son needing his camp paid up, she'd sent him back a note telling him to fuck off. That wasn't very sisterly of her, and he'd been pissed when he'd had to pay it himself. Then he'd heard from Maddie that she'd done the same thing to her about the ballet lessons that her kid had signed up for.

"It's not like we make her take them to the lessons. The least she could do is pay up. What sort of aunt is she trying to be? The deadbeat kind? Christ, I hate paying for those things, and when I had to shell out the two hundred and fifty bucks for it, I couldn't even reach her to ask her when she was going to pay me back." Sam had told Maddie that he'd tried calling her too, but nothing. "What sort of burr does she have up her ass now? I mean, she doesn't have any children. The least she could do is be the good aunt that she was in the past, don't you think?"

"Yes, I'm going to get to the bottom of this. There is no reason for her to be rude." He'd looked at the stack of things his kids were wanting money for and shook his head. "If I had known that she was going to be so slow in paying these things, I wouldn't have given them my phone number, but hers instead. That way they could hound her to death like they are me. What do these people think, that we're made of money? Damn it, she's going to have to get on the ball before they turn me over to a collection agency. And that will really piss me off."

"It doesn't work either; what I mean is, giving them her number won't work." He asked Maddie what happened. "She's changed the number. I have no idea why. She's probably trying to avoid some of those telemarketers or bill collectors. I'm telling you right now, Samuel, I'm not going to pay these for her. She needs to learn her responsibility when it comes to her nieces and nephews. What else is she going to spend the money on anyway?"

His wife had pointed out that she might stop paying for their things someday. What if she has her own kids? she'd asked him. Then what would they expect her to do? He'd told her that she'd have to learn to budget her money better. His wife was forever taking Sunny's side on things. Like Mary didn't think that she had any responsibility to provide for his kids.

"Yes, well, what sort of things are *we* going to be required to shell out for when she has kids?" He asked Mary what she meant. "She's paying for our children because they're her nephews. And Maddie's because they're her nieces. What about when she has some kids? Then what will we have to pay out?"

"I don't know where you come up with this shit. Do you really think she'd have a family? Christ, she can barely afford things our kids need. This is nothing to be bringing up right now, Mary. She's behind, and that's what we should be focusing on. And besides, Sunny won't marry. She cannot stand children. Just look how she acts around ours." Mary had agreed she was less than the sweet aunt that she had hoped for around their boys. "In addition, she might marry, but having children won't be a part of it. She isn't mother material."

Then a short month later he'd called his boss and let him know that he'd seen her in the plant snooping around. He'd only meant to get her into trouble for refusing, once again, to pay for things that his children were in. So when the opportunity had been placed before him to kill her off, he'd jumped at the chance. One less thing he'd have to worry about. And the three million that he had been promised from Alfred was more than enough to pay for anything that might come up regarding his children. Then there was the insurance he was going to collect on. Besides, he'd already planned on having the kids cut the shit down now that he was forking out the dough for it all. No more extra classes, dances, or anything now. He wanted to save what he had, not pay out for shit that wouldn't do any of them a dammed bit of good in their lives.

Putting the pictures away when someone knocked at his door, he smiled at Samuel Junior, his oldest son, when he entered the office. He plopped down on the chair and looked so lost that Sam wanted to get up and make it all right for him. But he waited for his son to tell him so that he could go and conquer the dragons, so to speak.

"The other boys in my class are going on a ski trip next month. I've tried getting in touch with Aunt Sunny, but her number isn't right." Sam told him that her number had been changed. "You told me that I should call her from now on when there were things that I needed, and I can't, Daddy. She has to pay for it. I don't want to be the only one left behind when they go off on this trip."

"I'm sure we can work out something." Samuel smiled at him, so much like his mother's smile. "In the meantime, you rest assured that I will try and find her number for you so you can call. You'll be going even if I have to go with her to write the check."

Samuel left a few minutes later with a big smile and an empty promise. There wasn't going to be any skiing trip... he wasn't going to pay for it, and neither was his dearly departed sister. She wasn't going to be paying for anything from now on. Laughing, Sam locked the drawer and went back to watch television with his family. Knowing that things would work out for the best, he actually enjoyed the movie and the company.

~~~

The house was huge, but it was the kitchen that she loved the most. Sunny wandered around the vast room and touched the granite countertops, the stove that had six burners, as well as the controls on the huge refrigerator. When David laughed, she felt like she'd been caught doing something wrong and glared at him.

"There are supplies if you want to cook dinner. I can see that you're just itching to make something." She nodded, feeling out of her element with such a good looking man. "I don't cook. It's not that I can't, I just don't. While there is an occasion that I can grill me a steak or something, I rarely do it. So if you want, go right ahead."

"I don't want to impose." She backed up when he moved toward her. The way he moved, gliding across the floor, made her itchy, like she was too big in her skin. "You don't need to get so close. And you are forever touching me. The others too, but they're used to it."

"Oh, but I think I do need to touch you. Not only that, but I would very much like to kiss you again." She pursed her lips. "How about you kiss me then? I'm not one of those men who has to be in charge all the time. I would love to once in a while, but right now, you can take the lead."

"I'd like to lead you to the deepest hole I can find and leave you there. You're a smartass; has anyone pointed that out to you? I'm betting they all do. Come to think of it, I think there is a bit of smartass in all of you." He laughed as he touched her cheek. "You're very touchy/feely, aren't you? Why can't you just leave your hands to yourself?"

"Because touching you gives me such a thrill. All the way to my cock." When he rolled his hips toward her, she felt just how much of a thrill he was getting. "What if I asked you if I could sit you on this counter and have my way with you? Would you enjoy that as much as I would?"

"I thought you were hungry." He growled that he was and nipped at her throat. "I can't think when you're doing that. Stop it. Why do you have to make things so ha...difficult all the time?"

"I don't want you to think, Sunny. I want you to feel, all of me. And I am hard as stone. Just thinking of taking you has me so close to the edge that I hurt with it." His hands were everywhere, and she was very much enjoying it. When he lifted her onto the counter, she looked down her body, then at him. She was topless, and her pants were unbuttoned.

"This is going really fast." He told her not fast enough for him when he took her breast into his mouth. "Christ, yes."

He had the mouth of a pro. As he suckled at her, massaging her breasts while he feasted on them, Sunny held him to her. She wasn't even sure that she could have pushed him away, not and live. He was that good.

"Do you have any idea what your scent is doing to me? It's like I can smell you on my clothing. I need to drink from you." She thought he meant bite her, but when he pulled her pants off, tearing them from her, she felt her pussy flood with cream. "Open for me, love. We need you."

The cat was there, his paws on either side of her thighs. The thought of running, hiding from him, was great, but then he licked her thigh and she nearly came from that alone. When he dropped to his feet, she started to move when he licked her pussy. Sunny came hard and fast.

"Whatever you did, you'd better do that again. Christ, that was heavenly." When she leaned back on the counter, opening her legs wider for his cat, his beast put his paws back on the counter and licked her. Sunny came twice more before he was able to press his tongue deep inside of her to fuck her that way.

The cat's tongue was rough to the point where she thought she'd be sore from it. But it was so blissful, it felt like her body was being worshiped. When the cat began to purr, Sunny felt it all the way to her toes…her pussy felt like it was being touched by a live wire. The best kind of vibrator, she thought.

When his cat let him go unexpectedly, he didn't pause where he'd left off but ate her as well. She screamed out his name when she came again and again. And when she jerked his head up from his meal, he grinned at her.

"Fuck me." He was naked, his cat having shredded his clothing, but he didn't need to be asked twice. Entering her forcefully, he paused when she wrapped her legs around him. "I need this. To come with you inside of me. I have no idea why…I don't even like you very much, but if you don't come inside of me soon, you'll be a dead kitty."

"I'm happy to oblige." He fucked her slowly, taking his time while his body got to know hers. "You're so tight around me. It's like you have me in your mouth."

"I'd like that too. Sucking you until you come down my throat. But it won't matter if you're dead." Laughing, he plucked her off the counter and took her to the living room, then the stairs. "Are you going to drop me off the edge?"

"No. Fuck you in our bed, where I have more room than on the counter." She squeezed him, her pussy tightening around him almost painfully. "You keep that up and we'll never make it."

They didn't, though that didn't stop them from fucking, because how they took each other wasn't making love, it was down and dirty. And it was amazing.

David took her on the stairs, the landing halfway up, as well as the wall outside their bedroom. Each time, she came hard enough to hurt herself. She knew that she'd be sore in the morning—hell, she was looking forward to being healed by his cat—but for now, the moment that they touched the bed, he made love to her like she meant the world to him. Which she supposed she did. Completing her world forever.

When she woke, he was curled around her. Her body was cool, so she pulled the blanket over them both. Holding him to her heart, a place that until now had been empty, she thought of what they'd just done. For someone taking it slowly, he certainly had rocked her world. When she spoke, he didn't say anything but held her to him.

"The cup that you had me touch belonged to a young slave. Not of the household, but he was abusive to her. She had three children by the man that she had worked for, but he'd taken them away when they were born. She was sure that he killed them all. Or sold them off at auction. It was common then to do that, but she believed that he did it so that no one would know they were his children." He asked if she knew the name. "Yes, she was simply called Apollo. The woman that served her the tea was someone by the name of Esther. They respected and loved one another for a very long time."

"Esther McFarland owned the house that my brother lives in. Dylan and he had been doing some extensive work on it before the servants' rooms were found." She told him that Apollo didn't live up there, but she did keep the others that worked there in line. "So, she was the head mistress."

"Sort of. The people that lived up there weren't just the hired help, because they were paid a good wage, but they were in training for another house when they left there. Job skills, I guess you could call it. When they were trained well enough, they'd send them to a free home where they could work and have their own things." Sunny sat up. "So much information, don't you think? I mean, all I did was touch it, and it's like this information flooded my mind."

"I thought you'd just get a name, not all this. Did you get much more?" She laughed when he sat up. "You can wait until tomorrow to tell me. When you asked to process it earlier, I didn't expect you to be up all night with it."

"I didn't expect to be made love to like that either, so I guess we both might as well be happy with the results." David kissed her after she moved to lie beside him. "Apollo could read and write. There's a book somewhere in the house that she hid away, just in case the authorities came to search the place. It has the names of families that were on the route out."

"I think we have that. Esther gave it to a friend of mine." Sunny nodded. "The cup and saucer, there are more that we have. Do you think if you touched them, you could get as much information from them?"

"I don't know. I mean, it doesn't exhaust me or anything like it did with Dylan. That was scary. But when I touched the cup you had, it was like I connected to the other woman, like we were sitting at a table and talking about her life. I could even ask her questions. By the way, she's buried out behind the barn. There are several graves out there; all of them are marked with a large stone that is planted in the ground."

He'd not known that, she thought. But then, it wasn't anything that Apollo had written down. The slaves were to be buried in mass graves without markers or fanfare. It was the way things were done. As he laid there, thinking of the graves, she wondered what Dylan or Evan would want to do about that. Sunny asked him if he was all right.

"Yes. I'm...I was thinking of my brother. Wondering if he'd want to do something with the graves. Mark them better or something." Sunny yawned, and David kissed her. "We can finish this up in the morning. You need your rest if you're going to ride me when we wake up."

Laughing, she curled around his body and held him. His soft breath blew over her hair for several minutes before she realized he was sound asleep. Closing her eyes, Sunny joined him in slumber.

Chapter 5

Alfred kept his tongue behind his teeth as he'd been instructed to do by his attorney. He wouldn't steer him wrong, being that they both had a great deal to lose if he was convicted. Of course, they had taken his business from him, but that wasn't too bad. He had enough money stashed away that once he was free, he'd be able to run just about anywhere. And he was headed right to a place that didn't have extradition laws. Looking at the mike that was shoved in his face for the umpteenth time since he'd been brought out of the courthouse, Alfred wanted to bite the top off the fucking thing and spit it at the woman holding it there.

"Mr. James, can you tell us where Miss Davis is? Did you pay to have her killed?" He stared at the woman who had just hit the very nail on the head he'd been trying to avoid. "She's been missing for several weeks now, and there is speculation that you've done something to her. Did you?"

He wanted to tell her that he had. That he'd not only paid to have her murdered, but he'd paid her own brother to do it.

And that the man had gotten off on it. Several times, according to the devices that he'd had planted in his home. Alfred even had a copy of the key Sam had made for the bottom drawer of his desk that he thought no one knew about. But he did... and not only that, Alfred had made sure that there were more pictures in inside than he'd thought.

Alfred could have told her that not only did he have that information, but that he'd had more evidence planted in the home of the brother that, if he decided to get stupider, would put him away for a very long time. That he had the gun that had killed her, the recording of the event, as well as some pretty damning information that should place the blame away from Alfred, should it come to that.

"My client has nothing to say about such accusations. If you don't mind, and you have nothing further to add to this, we'd like to get out of here."

Alfred followed his attorney and watched his face as he was put back into the police van and taken away. They'd talk, but not so anyone could hear them. *She's very smart, Miss Cummings is. We need to take care that she isn't nearly as smart as she believes herself to be. This could go bad quickly, Ralph. I want things to go in my direction again. What are you going to do about it?*

I'm working round the clock now. I have things going in our direction, as you called it, as we speak. A little accident here, a few minor hits to her lifestyle there. The little attorney won't know what hit her in a few weeks. That's all we need, her to look bad.

Alfred was a human and would remain so, but his attorney, Ralph Michael, wasn't. He was a wolf, one that had bitten him a few years ago so that they could have conversations like this when necessary. As much as he hated to admit it, they'd been using this little trick more and more lately. Things were that bad, thanks wholly to Sunshine Davis.

Hold off until she's close to closing this deal. I want her to feel the disappointment like a burn to her ass when fucked by someone bigger. He laughed at his own joke. *Any word on Davis? That fucking idiot brother of hers is going to pay as well. To think that I thought him too stupid to try and scam me.*

I have his bank records, as well as a few pictures of him and his lover. She's not talking, but then I don't think she can think beyond anything someone tells her to think. Dumber than a box of dead rats. He'd thought that about Sam too, but look where that had gotten him. *What do you want me to do now? I'm coming to the jail, but we can't talk around anyone there. What kind of books or shit can I bring you?*

The paper. Ralph said he'd get it and asked about anything else. *Yes, I'd very much like to have a good meal. See about getting one of the guards to let me have something from Franko's. I'm thinking you could have a nice dinner flown to me by dinner, can't you?*

I can if I can find the right man. By the way, there is some talk that you're going to be moved. They're saying that the jury pool in this area is going to be prejudiced against you. They're so stupid that I wonder how they even remember to eat. Of course it's prejudiced. You've paid most of them off before and threatened the others. But I'm not worried about having you moved to another place. It won't be an issue either. I have enough cash to take care of about any place they take you. That's what he paid the man for, to make sure this sort of thing was taken care of. *And you should know that I have a handle on what might have snatched up our girl's body. And where she's buried now. I'll know more in the morning. Just keep cool and let me handle things for you, Alfred. That's what you pay me for.*

After closing the connection before he arrived at the jail, he walked in without speaking to anyone. There were reporters there as well, waiting like vultures to get a piece of him. But Alfred had learned a long time ago that less was more. And in this case, keeping his mouth shut was the best way to deal with these morons. Also, he'd learned that they would take things and stretch them out to be nothing at all like he'd said them. Putting a swing on things that would make him look a great deal worse than he was. Well, in most people's eyes, anyway.

His cell had been upgraded to a nice-looking hotel suite. Not that he'd not had to pay out the ass for the few luxuries that he had, but it was nice not to have to put up with cotton sheets and an exposed commode.

As he sat down behind his desk to check on his email, he looked up when someone said his name. The woman standing there didn't look familiar, so he returned to his work.

"If you've come here to ask me questions, I'm going to have to refer you to my attorney. Anything else you want from me...." He looked her up and down and found her to be quite beautiful. "Well, I'm sure we can work something out that will be advantageous to us both."

"Nah, I figured out that your attorney is just as crooked as you are. So, whatcha got planned for your defense? You figuring that out while you sit in here in your cushy little cell? Just curious, do you get five star rated food too? And someone to come in and put a little mint on your pillow at turn down time?" He looked at her. "Oh, I am supposed to tell you that you're being recorded. But a man like you, you'd probably know that already."

He looked up at the camera in the corner. It had been turned off a few hours after he'd gotten there. Not saying anything to her, he laughed when the door at the end of the hall was opened and two of his men, officers on his payroll, came in. Two more joined them, dressed in suits. He looked at the woman again.

"What's this all about? I'm not doing a damned thing to anyone. Minding my own business, making sure that I put the lid up on the commode when I piss." She smiled at him, and he felt as if she'd slapped him. "Who the fuck are you?"

"First things first, shall we? These officers have confessed to all kinds of shit they've been doing for you. I've made arrangements for them to be in the cells next to yours. These other men, the guys with me, are here to strip you of your little toys and then put you in a nice orange suit. If you don't do it yourself, that is." He asked her who she thought she was. "Dylan Whitfield. Special agent to the United States of America, and your worst nightmare all rolled up with a nice little bow for you. So if you're a smart cookie, at least as smart as you think you are, you'll play nicely. Or not. I'd actually like for you not to. It'll make my job more fun."

The suits unlocked his cell and told him to stand up. The men that he'd been paying were put in the cell across from him and to his right. Cooperating with the men was his best bet right now, so when he was told to put his hands over his head, he did so as he was lowered none too gently to the floor. His things were pulled out as he was read his rights again.

"You do have a lot of pretty little things in here, don't you, Alfred? But I don't see any photos of the family. You do have one, don't you?" She laughed. "Oh, that's right. They ran off. Left you in that big house of yours all alone. Which,

I almost forgot to mention, is being searched too. As well as the other *safe* houses that you own. That safe you have? Nice, but you really should take care to have a better combination for it. They had that fucker cracked in less than ten minutes."

"What is the meaning of this? You have no right to come in here and take my things from me. I have a written letter from the governor of this state saying that I can have a bit of extra because of who I am. And you'd better be producing a search warrant for the search of my other homes too, young lady." She said nothing as the men, three more who had come in after the first ones, moved out his desk and started cataloging everything in it. "Answer me, damn it."

"The meaning of this is that you've been paying off the men that work here for your own personal gain. I'm pretty sure that it's only the tip of the iceberg in shit you've been doing. But that got me a good look into other things you might be getting, and thanks for the heads up. Being recorded and all, you telling me where you got your special permission helps even more. So, the governor that has so nicely given you this useless piece of paper, he's in jail too, but in a bigger one than you have. Make you jealous? As for your rights? You left them at the doorstep the second you fucked around in my state. Also, I don't like you. Not a biggie when it comes to the number of people that don't like you, but mine has a bit more of a bite. Do you feel it yet, Alfie?"

"I demand that you call someone and get this fixed. I will not be treated this way." Dylan laughed. "You're going to pay for this. I swear to you, if it's the last thing I do, you're going to pay."

"You're threatening a federal officer, mister. I'd be careful of what you spew from those lips of yours."

He wanted her dead and reached to Ralph to have him do it.

I can't talk to you right now. He asked him why the fuck not. *Because my alpha is here, and he's going to kill me for helping you.*

You tell him that I'll pay him whatever he wants. Ralph laughed. *What the fuck is so funny?*

I'm a dead man. It's been good, Alfred.

The sound of Ralph's scream in his mind made Alfred's head hurt badly. And when he tried reaching for him again, all he got was dead air, like he'd been hung up on. Alfred had a feeling that the woman was right...this was only the tip of the fucking iceberg, and his ship was going down fast.

~~~

Dylan was glad to do this. It should have been done a long time ago, but she was happy she could do it now. As the furniture was moved out of the cell, each item put to paper and numbered, she thought of the things they'd found that were potentially dangerous for a great many people. Especially for Sunny. The cell phone and computer not even the half of it.

Sunny's brother was involved. And he was in so deep that it looked as if he might be the next one she went to visit. Her cell started ringing just as the large area map and pins stuck in it were being removed.

"How's it going?" She told Henry, the president, what she'd found so far. "All that? I'm assuming that the force there is corrupt."

"You have no idea. Once we caught the two that we knew of, it started to fall like a tumble of bricks. And not only does the police force here need to be jailed and replaced, but about every official here, including the clergy at the local boys' club." He asked her what was going on there. "Money being misused. Food for the homeless missing. I have more units going over books here than you have on staff there. This is a fuck storm. To be honest, I'm even surprised at not just how deep this goes, but who is involved. It's scary."

"Did you find anything out about Sunshine? I know that was one of the reasons that you wanted to go." Dylan told him what she'd discovered. "I see. Her own family turned against her. It's far worse than you thought, isn't it?"

"Yes. Sunny said she thought it was her brother that had shot her. I think she was saying it that way because she didn't want to believe that it was him. So far I've not found anything out about her sister, though she's just as much of a fucking cunt as the brother is a prick. I've not had to do more than ask about Maddie, and I'm getting all kinds of stories from neighbors and people that she goes to the club with. I'm getting shit together to go see her next. I have a feeling that my work here is going to extend for a few states. I guess Maddie is on the board of directors at the private school where her kids attend, and they want her gone so badly that I think any or all of them would have paid me to end her life. And she's on the board at the country club. As soon as I ask to see their books, I have a feeling that they're going to turn them over, and her, before I finish saying I have a warrant. She's as bad as Sunny is nice."

"You do what you need to out there and I'll back you up. We want Sunny safe and sound. I've been reading over some of the articles that she's done, and she's brilliant. The chemical lab story alone will save countless lives now that it's no longer operational. My God, Hutch, she's a value to us all." Dylan told him to her family as well. "Yes, I'm so glad that she's with young David. I think the two of them will be wondrous. How is our new governor getting along? Has he gotten any better at taking credit for things he's done himself?"

"If Lily, his secretary, has anything to do with it, I think when you're finished there, she'll have him in the White House so fast that he won't know how it happened." They both laughed, and one of the officers came to show her something. "I have to go, sir. There is too much going on here for me to be shooting the shit with you."

"All right then. Call me if you need me. You know that I'm here for you. And if you have any trouble getting paperwork, let me know. I've been known to kick a few doors in for you." She said she knew that. "Oh, and I might have just the person in line for that area. I'll let you know."

It took them the better part of eight hours to get things squared away. There were things in his cell that would be very helpful in convicting the force here, as well as some things that she knew would help with the case against Samuel Davis. The guy was bad news.

As much as she wanted to go out and find the fucker now, she knew that it had to be done in an orderly way. Otherwise he'd walk. But she could put out a few things, someone to follow him, another person to look into his life, which would make it easier. And she had to tell him, and this fucker here, that they'd missed the boat in taking Sunny out of the picture. Sunny had agreed.

"Once he finds out that he's got me around, what is it you think he'll do?" Dylan started to reply, but Sunny answered her own question. "He'll come after me. To finish the job and to shut me up. It'll matter little to him that I'm still alive, he'll just want to finish the job. And I just found out today when I changed my insurance around, Sam has been asking questions on how he can make himself my beneficiary. The fucking ass. He has to know that I remember who it was that shot me, and that's not going to go over well, I don't think."

"Doubtful. He's a moron if he thinks that you're going to just lie low. You're not, are you?" Sunny said she wouldn't. Actually, she said fuck no, but either way, it told her what she wanted to hear. "You just stay put out there and don't come out here. Once he is told, which I'm going to do all on my own, he might get a little stupid."

"Stupider. He's never been one that was very smart." They both laughed. "You be careful. I know you're this bad ass leap leader and all, but you can still get hurt, and he will try."

"I'm as careful as I ever am." Sunny said to be more so. "All right, Mommy, I will be careful. But you do the same. You and I, we're going to be working together, I hope, and I don't want David to come and try and kick my ass."

"I'll kick yours if you get so much as a hangnail from this shit. Sam's not smart, but he's going to want to cover his own ass in this, and killing anyone that might be involved in his fuck up, that'll be high on his list of shit to get done." Dylan had agreed with her. "And my sister...she's a viper, and just as deadly. I have never seen her lose it, but I know that she can. So watch her like you would a deadly snake."

Dylan got a call from the alpha in this area, and he simply told her that she could come to Ralph's home now. No one would be bothering with it. Dylan thanked him and he laughed.

"No worries, my dear. I'm going to have to find us another attorney now, but I think I'll be smarter about it this time. I have a feeling that the pack is going to be finding out a lot of things that we didn't know about him." She told him she was sorry. "Nothing to be sorry about. You more than likely saved us a great deal of grief. I would ask if you find anything about us, such as pictures or notes, that you allow me to have those. I don't need that falling into the wrong hands, as you can well imagine."

"Yes, I understand. I'd like to suggest to you that he has a fire sale." He laughed. "Once we're both satisfied that his house is clean, then we can roast a few marshmallows around the fucker. That way, no one but the two of us, and a few of my men who you can trust, will know what happened there. All right?"

"You know, I do like your style of thinking. Yes, I believe that will be a splendid way to end his reign over corrupt doings." He laughed again. "If you ever come this way on a social visit, though why you'd do that is beyond me, you look us up. I'd love to meet your mate. He must be a strong man to let his wife become the leap leader."

"He is the very best there is. And I'll tell him that. Thank you for your help." He said it was his pleasure. "You need anything, let me know. I have connections."

They were in the hotel at around midnight when she got a second call from Sunny. She was coming to them. Dylan thought it a perfect idea, and told her that she'd wait for her. To have her brother and sister face to face with Sunny might be the best thing for her. And if things got out of hand, she'd kill them. Her or Sunny actually, but she knew that they could should it become necessary. Dylan really liked her new sister-in-law.

As soon as they hung up after making arrangements to

meet up, David contacted her.

Do you think she'll be all right? Facing them, I mean? She's been waffling about it all day, and only just now decided to do this. Dylan told him that she'd be better for this. *Yeah, well, I don't want her hurt again. I mean, I couldn't have stopped it from going on before, but this time I can. And killing him will be my greatest pleasure.*

Not for her. If it comes to that, you let someone else do it. He asked why. *Regardless of what he's done to her, he's still her brother. And no matter what, he'll remain so. If you do this, she might be happy for it, but it will be there in her head for the rest of your lives together that you killed him. Let the pros take it. I'm not saying that Samuel won't have to be put down like the dog that he is, but don't you do it unless you absolutely have to. Promise me that, David. I want you two to have a good start to your lives together, and that might not happen with this hanging over your head.*

Besides, she thought, Sunny might be the best person to kill the fucker once and for all. It would hurt her, of course, but it would also help her deal with what he'd done to her. The sister too. The more she found out about the duo, the more she thought that someone should have killed them long ago. Not hurt, that would be too nice, but to outright murder the fuckers.

Chapter 6

Madeline knocked on her brother's door again and waited for him to answer. The nerve of the dickweed to have invited her over then not be there. Of course, she was an hour early, but that didn't mean he shouldn't have been up and going by now.

She looked at him when he finally answered. He'd only just rolled out of bed. And not only that, but he smelled too, like he'd been on a bender and was just now getting home. But instead of pointing out the obvious, like he should take better care of himself, she told him what she thought.

"I've been standing out here forever, Samuel. What are you still doing in your bed clothing? I thought you wanted to talk to me. You sent me a message, telling me to come here to talk to you. And you couldn't have taken a moment to have told me that you were running behind?" He looked at her again, then simply walked away to sit on the stairs. "Samuel, what do you want? I have a meeting at one, and I must get ready for it. They're asking questions at the school and the

67

country club. I don't have time for this."

"I didn't message you, Maddie. And why would you even think I'd have you come over here at such an ungodly hour? Christ, it's not even seven yet, and you're going on like a harpy. Just shut up and let me wake the fuck up. I don't suppose since you came here to bother me that you brought over some coffee and a Danish, did you?" She pulled out her phone to show him that he had too messaged her to come here. As far as bringing him something, she didn't even justify that with a response. He knew how she felt about such things. "The boys were invited to this thing at the school, and since it was free, we let them go. Without our benefactor around, I don't feel like shelling out money for every little thing they want."

"My children were invited to something too. How odd. Anyway, you did too message me. I have it right here." She showed him the message and then moved to the dining room. She could smell food in there, and since she'd messed up her day for him, he was going to feed her.

Madeline nearly fell back when she saw Sunshine sitting at the table having breakfast. Madeline decided to play this cool. Sunshine shouldn't be there. Not only that, but the fact that she was up and around was also something that shouldn't be going on. Samuel had told Madeline that he killed Sunny. Shot her full of so many holes that she was dead before he got to have his fun. Now this.

"I've been trying to reach you. Where have you been? There are things going on that you've neglected." She looked to her right when Sunshine did and saw that Samuel had joined them. She could see on his face that he was just as surprised as she'd been, if not more. "What is wrong with you now? You said she'd come back. Well, gather up the things you wanted to talk to her about. I have mine right here. These should have been paid weeks ago, Sunshine. I can't believe that you'd not have taken care of these things before running off to God knows where."

Madeline winked at him, trying to show him that he had to pretend that he'd done nothing wrong. Shit like this could get them both in trouble. Well, not her...she'd not done a damned thing to her sister. But if Samuel wanted to, he could and would make trouble for her. He was too stupid to lie well. But Sunshine spoke before she could make Samuel understand.

"I'm not going to be paying anything, if that's what you have to gather up. I thought I made that clear when I left here. You had those kids. I didn't mind being the nice person and paying some things, but I think we both know that I've gone well beyond the norm when it comes to being money bags for them. Hello, Sam. What's happening in your life?" He stumbled to the chair just as a man came from the kitchen with two glasses. "This is my husband, David Whitfield. David, this is my brother and sister, the ones I was telling you about. Sam, are you unwell?"

"I.... How did you get here?" She told him that she drove, like most people did. "No. I mean...where have you been all this time? Surely you could have called us. You've seen the newspaper, wondering where you were. And since you changed your phone number, we couldn't get in touch with you. That's bad form, Sunny, even for you."

"I suppose that I could have contacted you, but this is so much more fun. Have a seat, the two of you. I have a few things to say." She looked at her husband. "Did you get the recipe for the scones? I think that Beth could make these for us, don't—?"

"I demand to know what the hell you're doing here, Sunny." Madeline looked at her brother, and then at Sunshine. He was blowing this. Stepping up to the table, she sat in the chair that was as far as she could get from any of them. Samuel continued just as she was seated. "What I mean is, how did you get in my house? Don't you believe in letting anyone know that you're here?"

Madeline wasn't going to get caught here, not with Sunshine knowing that Samuel had shot her. What did she hope to gain by coming here, unless she had the police with her? It wouldn't surprise her if she did. Sunshine was cunning like that. Samuel looked at her then at Sunshine.

"I knocked and Hans let me in, he even asked me if I wanted to have something to eat, which I accepted. We had a nice long talk, you see, and he's been so nice. As for letting you know where I was? You of all people, Sam, should have had a little clue where I might have been. Don't you think? I mean, we did see each other right before I disappeared. Remember?"

"I don't know what you're talking about. You've been gone for a very long time, that's all I was saying." He laughed, but Madeline thought it sounded very forced. "So, now that you're here, what do you say we all have dinner together? Get to know the new man in your life."

"He's my husband, not some stranger I plucked from the streets. David and I are here on a mission, you might say. And there won't be time for dinner, for either of you." Madeline asked her why not. "Oh, this and that. By the way, just to give you a heads up, Sam, I think the police want to speak to you about a few things."

Sunshine was being very coy or very smart. Her attitude about this was affecting Samuel, and when he was nervous or afraid, he couldn't maintain his level of coolness like she could. Yes, he was going to get them both in trouble at this rate. Madeline hated not being able to tell him to shut up before he said something that got them into trouble. What could the police possibly want with Samuel? It wasn't as if Sunshine was actually dead, was she? Other than attempting to kill her, they didn't have anything on him. But it would be Samuel's and her word against their sister. And anyone who knew Sunshine knew her to be a flake and a fool. Madeline intended to find out what they had on him and help him. But before she could ask, Hans, her brother's butler, came in to hand Samuel an envelope.

"This is my resignation, sir. You will also be receiving the rest of the household's before the end of the day, via email, I believe." Hans looked at Sunshine, who was smiling like a loon. "Thank you, my lady. I do hope you have a very wonderful new life. You deserve it."

"Thank you, Hans. And my offer to you still stands. Just let me know—"

"What the fuck is going on here? Hans, you're not going anywhere. And the rest of my staff had better not be leaving either." Hans left them, and Madeline heard the front door open and close. Madeline stood, then sat again when Sunshine told her to. "You will not speak to me like that. I'm older than you, and you'll remember that."

"Oh, I remember it. Very well, as a matter of fact. And whatever you say, you should know that you're being recorded. Every word, every syllable. Also, your home will soon be cleared out as well. The police again. They've been there since you left your house early this morning. Randal has been most helpful in that area. Same as Mary has been. They are being investigated as well, but I don't think we'll have much on them, do you?" Sunshine pushed her plate back and smiled. "From now on, you will have someone keeping an eye on you both."

Sunshine and her pretend husband stood up and moved toward the door. There wasn't any way they were leaving there until Madeline had answers, and money. When she stood up again, Sunshine just stared at her before looking at Samuel.

"Sam, you should know that the police found some records on your buddy that will show up soon. Also, Alfred has been moved to another cell, his phone taken from him, as well as his computer. As yours has been as well. I would guess that, like your office computer, it has all sorts of information on it that will help the police in their investigation." Sunshine looked at Madeline. "Your home, as we speak, is also being looked over, as I said earlier. As well as the company computers at the club, and the boards that you use when you go there. You two have a lovely day."

When she was gone, Madeline looked at Samuel. He was sobbing. Crying like a little baby with great gulps of air. Not understanding why he wasn't fighting back, or at least saying something, she jerked his head up by his hair and told him to tell her what the fuck he was going to do now. He cried harder, but nodded.

"I killed her." Madeline told him she knew that. "But she's not dead. She's here. Sunny was right here in my house. I shot her several times and left her for dead. And now, here she is and she knows it all."

"You obviously didn't kill her, so that isn't anything you should concern yourself with. Also, what would she know? Sunshine only knows what we want her to know, you know that." She stood up and went to the sideboard, and noticed that the food there had been drowned in catsup, a condiment that she despised. "I hope there is more than this to eat, Samuel. And I don't know what's up Hans's, ass but you'd better nip this quitting thing in the bud now. Or you're going to be sorry trying to run this house without anyone's help."

There was nothing in the kitchen for her to eat, and the hot tea machine had been turned off some time ago so the water was now cold. She looked around the large room, not having been in there for a very long time, and wondered what Sunshine had been talking about. Her house was off-limits to people. And she'd have the head of anyone that went in without her permission.

Going back to the dining room, she had Samuel get dressed so that he could take her out to eat. The very least that he could do was feed her since he'd called her there. Or did Sunshine do that? Whatever, she was hungry and he was paying for it.

~~~

Sunny leaned into the commode and threw up again. Christ, she knew that she shouldn't have eaten, but at the time, it was eat or kill her family. When someone said her name, she groaned when Dylan joined her in the public bathroom.

"Go away." Dylan laughed and sat on the counter when Sunny turned to lean against the wall. "I did just what you said. I don't think it helped at all."

"Oh, but it did. You scared the fuck out of Sam. By the

way, why does your sister call you both by your given name? And, we did find enough shit on them both to put them away for a while. Your sister is as bad as your brother." Sunny nodded, but decided that if she did that again her head was going to come off. "You okay now?"

"No, I'm not sure I ever will be again. As for Maddie and our names, she has it in her head that shortened names for us is vulgar. Her kids' names aren't shortened either. I do it, but only to piss her off." Dylan laughed. "Have you really gone to my sister's house too?"

"Yes." When she left it at that, Sunny decided that she really didn't want to know. "Are you ready for some information, or do you want to wait until you're up and moving?"

"Is it bad?" Dylan nodded. "Then tell me now, that way if it makes me sick again, I'm close enough to get to a commode. Hans did quit. So, did the rest of the staff. I was joking when I told Maddie hers did as well."

"They've been taken into custody to keep them safe and to answer a few questions. So, you didn't lie to her. And Hans, he's a nice man, by the way, and is being very cooperative too." Sunny got up and washed her hands. Dylan continued. "Two weeks ago, your brother-in-law filed for divorce, and he is going to get it. Also, your sister-in-law, Mary, did the same thing. While the two of them are not having an affair, they have been talking a great deal, and decided that something was going on and they were getting out. Neither of them have anything to add to the cases against your siblings. The children will be questioned too, but gently, and then if all goes like I think it will, they'll go back to your in-laws. But your sister and brother will be going to prison. Things are well beyond what we thought they were. Okay so far?"

"And the kids? What will they know? I mean, they'll be questioned, so how much will they have to know about their parents?"

Dylan said she didn't think any of the children had been happy for some time. "And, while the other parent was in the clear, they are going to lose everything they held near and dear. Everything they have will be taken." Sunny said she had been paying for most of their shit anyway. "Yes, we know. And that will all be returned to you as well. I have a very good attorney on your side, and he's going to have your name put high on the list of people to be paid back. From the estate. There won't be any cash that they can touch."

"Good. While I don't understand them, the kids might make it out of this better off without my family around. What have you found out about my parents?" Sunny wasn't sure she wanted an answer to that part. She was terrified that either, or both, her brother and sister had killed them off. With all the stuff she'd been finding out about them, she wouldn't put it past them. There had been insurance on them both, doubled when they were killed like they were, but she wasn't sure how much that was. Sunny had been away when they had died, and the settlement that she'd received was still in her account.

"They died, as far as we can tell, just as you were told. They were staying at a nice hotel close to the water when the waves hit. A great many people died that way. As for bodies, there were never any recovered. I'm sorry." She nodded. "Sunny, you should know that your brother is going away for a very long time. Years, if not life. Maddie has been skimming the accounts at her husband's company and the country club where she's the treasurer. Those books are being looked at as well."

"Christ. Do either one of them have a decent bone in their body?" Dylan said that it didn't appear so. "I'm not sure I can take too much more of this. Is there anything pressing I need to deal with?"

"No, but I will tell you that we're not arresting either of them. We could...there is enough to bring them in with. But I thought, since they know you're around, that it would be much more fun to let them hang themselves a little more. You know, get them with their pants down around their ankles and then fuck them in the ass."

"You do have a way with words, don't you?" Dylan got off the counter and moved to the door. "Thank you for this. I'm not sure what might have happened had I not confronted them, but to see the look on Sam's face made being sick so much easier to deal with."

"Yes, that was priceless. And I'm glad you told them about being watched. That way we'll have a leg to stand on when this goes down, and it will." She nodded and followed her out of the bathroom. "How about we head over to the hotel, rest up a bit, then go out for dinner? Nothing that might make you ill again."

"Sure. Right now that doesn't sound appealing, but I'll be hungry soon. Besides, I have a couple of things I need to take care of before leaving here. I want to sell my home and deal with the furniture I have in storage." Dylan said she'd see her later and Sunny leaned into David's chest when he held her. "It's been a terrible day. I need something to do."

"Good, I have just the plan. After we deal with your house and things, we'll go to the zoo. I've not been to one in ages." Sunny thought he was kidding, but agreed that was a sound plan. "Then after that, I take you back to the hotel and ravish you. If you feel like it, we can have dinner."

"Dylan invited us to have dinner with her and Evan." He said that sounded good too. "I have some things in storage that were my parents'. I'd like to take them back to the house if we can."

"Yes, anything you want." They were headed to the car when she saw her sister and brother. Maddie was talking a mile a minute, and Sam looked as if he was being led around by a leash. "They're not going to be happy when they try to use their credit cards. And it's doubtful that either of them would stoop low enough to carry cash. Maddie thinks it's all covered in coke, and that one touch of it will make you an addict. Dylan told me that they had closed up the accounts and houses as soon as they could, along with their banks. Also, cars are being taken to see what sort of things are in them."

"They'll be broke in so many ways. I did manage to get some cash out of the accounts of both parents for the kids. And a nice hotel for a week." She thanked him for that. "You're so very welcome. And I love you, so it was easy to do."

"I'd love to be there." He pulled her along to the restaurant that they had entered. "You don't think this is going to cause a scene, do you? I mean, they'll know it was me that had something to do with this. I don't want other people's meals to be ruined because I'm wanting to see this happen to them."

"You didn't do anything but give them a heads up. They should have asked if they had questions about their finances. Besides, I'm betting that you're hungry after being sick in the bathroom. Come on, this'll be fun." They entered the place and were seated a few tables away from the other two. "This way we can watch and not be caught. I hope that this place has cameras."

An hour after they were served, Sunny knew that the card had been declined. It was followed by another ten minutes of loud voices, as well as crying...her brother, not Maddie. Maddie was making a scene now, telling anyone that would listen that the restaurant was doing this. Her credit and her brother's was just fine. But as soon as she saw her, Maddie came after her.

"You did this?" Sunny asked her what she'd done. "You had our cards cut off. Why would you do such a thing? I mean, it's bad enough that you left us holding the bag with all these fees and such, but to do this is reprehensible. Fix this, or so help me, Sunshine, I'll stick these cards down your throat until you choke to death on them."

"And how do you suppose I'm to do that, Maddie? Shit you a new card?" Maddie drew back to slap her. "You go ahead and do that. If you do, then I'm calling the cops and having you arrested for assault. If I don't hurt you first, and trust me when I tell you, I've had a lot of experience with bullies, and I won't hesitate to kick your ass all over this place."

"I'll get you back for this, Sunshine. See if I don't. And you can pick up the tab on this." When she started to walk away, Sunny laughed. "What the fuck is so funny? You won't laugh when I start having my bills sent to your home."

"Again, how do you think that's going to work, Maddie? I no longer live around here." She asked her where she was. "None of your business. You should also know that you're not going to be any happier when you go to the bank. That's cut off as well, Maddie. When you fuck up, you should know that eventually you're going to have to pay for it. I love that I got to be a part of it too, so you know."

"My name is Madeline." She even spelled it for her. "And we'll just see how much I get from my bank, Sunshine. I'm not one to fuck with. You'll learn that soon enough."

"Yes, so I've heard. You have a nice life, Maddie." As they finished up their meal, she looked at David. "I don't feel sick this time. Actually, I feel relieved. Thank you for doing this for me. I hate that she's made a scene, but to be honest, I feel wonderful now."

"Good. I have plans for you later."

They got up and left just as the police were pulling up. She could hear her sister telling the cops to stop them, but David just moved them along. By the end of the day, her sister would be in jail, she'd bet anything.

Chapter 7

David woke up at midnight, disoriented and confused. Realizing that he was in a hotel room helped, but he had no idea why he'd woken. Getting up quietly, so as not to disturb Sunny, he made his way to the living area and looked around. He was startled to see Tanner there.

"I've come to make sure that you're all right and to touch base with you. I'm to understand that you've confronted her sister and brother." David sat down and told him everything that had gone on earlier. "It's difficult to believe that they come from the same gene pool as Sunny. Is she all right?"

"Yes, very well. Confronting them on this level helped her more than anything else could have, I think. She is sleeping like a baby right now. And she's been working with me on the book, giving me an understanding that I never had before on some of the things I've found. You should see her work." He smiled. "Enough small talk. What's going on, really?"

"I am in need of a place to rest during the day. I know that I could purchase a home in town to be near you all, but it would raise suspicions, and I don't want to have to deal with that. I may later, but for now, I just wish to have a place that I can go to and not have to deal with anything or anyone that I don't want to. Should you two allow me to reside in your sublevels from time to time, I'll pay for the improvements that I will require, and make sure that you never worry over taxes and such."

"You're more than welcome to stay there. No cost, Tanner. You're a friend of the family, so I don't want you to feel like you must pay." He asked what Sunny would say. "You saved her life. I'm sure that she'll agree with me in that you will be a welcome guest. Have you been in the basement level? It's finished, but not very livable at the moment. I know that you could fix it up anyway that you want, and you should do that. Anything."

"Yes, I've been in the house before. A while ago. When it was being built, I found myself nearby when I needed to rest." He didn't ask, and Tanner didn't seem inclined to tell why he'd been in need of a place. "The book you are writing, I've found a couple of people that might be able to help you as well. Two of them were there when the slaves were hidden away, and one of them was a former resident and trained there to become a housemaid. Their numbers are on the table there."

David glanced in that direction, but didn't go to it. Tanner leaned back on the couch and closed his eyes. He would bet anything that the vampire wasn't sleeping, nor relaxed. When he spoke next, David was quiet.

"Two days ago I felt my mate. He was killed. It has broken me in ways that I cannot describe properly to you. I have...for lack of a better term, I've been in mourning. My kiss too, they're all dead. Killed when it came out that the lab was going to be overrun by the Feds. I should have looked then, when I had the address, but he was gone before I could get there." David told him he was sorry. "As am I. It was Alfred that did it. Not directly, but he was there all the same. I'm not sure that I have a reason to go on any longer. I won't bring harm onto your family with this, but I'd like for you to know."

"You will though." Tanner stood up when Sunny entered the room. David did as well, and held her hand when she sat next to him. "You'll go on living because I have a plan for you."

"Oh? And what plan, pray tell, do you have for an old queer vampire that you couldn't do yourself? I'm assuming that it has something to do with your powers." Sunny told him it didn't. "Then what, Sunny? I'm an old man who is tired of living alone and in darkness."

"I need you to help me with a few projects. As in, with this business that I'm starting up." This was the first that David had heard about it, but he kept his mouth closed while she continued. "I'm an investigative reporter that gets the job done. But there are times when I am going in blindly to a situation. You could help me with that."

"You mean scout ahead to keep you out of trouble? You have a tiger by the tail for that, my dear. You'll have to do better than that." She nodded and stood up. When she put out her hand to Tanner, he looked at her. "What?"

"You saved my life, correct?" He said that he had, but only because he needed her. "You still need me, Tanner, as much as I do you. Take my hand and we'll shake on being partners. And yes, I do have a tiger, but he's not trained to be stealthy, nor is his cat all that friendly when I get hurt. You might be upset, but you will do so with grace and calmness."

"I can be graceful and calm." David stood up and knocked an empty wine glass to the floor, where it shattered. "Usually, I'm graceful and calm."

They all laughed, but he was pretty sure that Sunny wasn't going to convince Tanner to stick around. When Tanner stood too, David thought he was going to leave without any sort of promise at all.

"And if I see that where you are headed is too dangerous for you, you'll heed my word? You'll stop and let me take care of you?" Sunny smiled. "That is no answer. It's more of a promise that you will tread where you shouldn't. Will you? I cannot be responsible for your safety if you don't listen to me, child. This cannot work if you are forever going full ahead, and me back behind you begging for you to be careful."

"All right then, I promise you that I will listen to you when you tell me it's too dangerous. But if there is trouble involving children that can't help themselves, then all bets are off. And so long as you aren't getting hurt either. Promise?" Tanner took her hand in his. "I think that was too easy. You were set to sit out in the sun or whatever it was you were planning, and now you're going to work with me. What gives?"

"I needed to be needed." She said that she could understand that. "Yes, I would imagine that you would. All right, partner, may I rest in your sublevels? And you'll tell me when you've had enough of me?"

"You can stay there for as long as you wish. Forever, should you want." The two of them hugged, and David let out a long breath that he'd not realized he'd been holding. They were together in this, and he was happy about it. "Tanner, I think that even had you not saved my life, we would still have been good friends. You're a wonderful person."

"Thank you, my dear. That means the world to me." He kissed her on the cheek before stepping back. "I shall go. I have myself a fae that works with me. She's old too, and very set in her ways. Do not call her a bug, for she will hurt you. Perhaps not you, but she will be most vexed. Her name is Flora."

It was late and early at the same time when Tanner left them. Going to breakfast seemed the best bet. That way they could get an early start on what their plans for the day was. Mostly it was putting her house on the market and going through it, as well as her storage unit, to see what she wanted to keep. It wasn't going to take long, and they made plans to head home afterwards.

They were just sitting down when Evan contacted him.

I'm telling you this so that you can talk to Sunny. Her brother is dead. He hung himself last night. David said nothing as Evan continued. *He left a note. It's a confession of sorts, but he doesn't mention trying to kill Sunny. He also said that he and Maddie have been in collusion for about ten years now in skimming the places where they work.*

Where did he do it? Evan told him that Sam had been taken into custody with his sister right after lunch. Something about an unpaid lunch bill and credit cards. *Maddie made bail, but he didn't. She offered to pay to have him released too, but he didn't want her to. He told her that he wanted to think. I think he figured that was the best place for him, seeing as how his attorney told him not long before that he was going to prison.*

I'll tell her all that. But we're headed home today. She has some things that she wants to take back with us, furniture and things of her parents. If you'd see to that, we'll rent us a car or something and leave you two the jet. Evan said to tell her that he was sorry. *I will. Thank you, Evan.*

After closing the connection, he looked at Sunny. She'd dealt with a lot of things over the last few days, and he hated to add to it. Taking her hand into his, he opened his mouth to tell her when she put her other hand over his mouth.

"He's dead, isn't he?" He asked her how she knew. "I don't know if you were aware of this, but Sam and I were twins. So, as much as I'd like to not believe in the connection, I think that's what woke me last night. Where is he now, and where did he do this? The jail?"

"Yes. He could have made bail, Maddie offered to pay, but he said that he wanted some time alone to think. Evan seems to think that he knew he was going to prison, and didn't think that he'd make it on the inside." He held her hand as she sat there, crying softly. "I'm so sorry, love. We can stay another day if you want."

"No. I mean, he and Maddie made it perfectly clear what they thought of me. And while I'm broken that he's dead, I don't think that I'll be terribly welcomed into this journey, do you?"

"No, I wouldn't imagine so. He left a note." She said that she didn't want to talk about it now, and David said he was all right with that. "Are you still wanting to go to the house and storage? We can go on home if you wish."

"We'd have to come back. No, let's just get this done so we don't have to. All right? I want to just go home and not think about things here for the rest of my life." He said that was fine by him. "I'm assuming that I'm going to have to deal with his estate too, aren't I?"

"Yes. Mary filed for a divorce, so she won't be able to

make decisions for him. But nothing can be done until things are settled with the trial anyway." She nodded and told him she loved him. "And I love you, Sunshine. So very much. We'll get through this."

"I know, but it's all so wrong, on so many levels." He agreed. "All right. My house, and then to the storage place. After that, whatever you want to do. I'm ready to do something constructive."

So was he. As they made their way to her home, he thought about Sam and Maddie. They were the worst family members he'd ever run across, and now one of them was dead. He wanted to shake off the dust of this town too.

~~~

Tanner loved the openness of the sublevels in David's home. He could make this work, and was glad that he was going to be working with the young woman too. As he made arrangements to have some of his things brought here for him to use, he wondered if either of them would care if he did a few improvements on their security.

They already had a state of the art system, but he wanted something more. Something that he, as a vampire, would need. Calling to his day walker, she moved into the space with him. Flora didn't look like the typical day walker, not being a fae. She was beautiful, with bright golden hair and wings that made you think of treasure chests full of coins. And she was very tiny.

"They have flowers here. Did you see them?" He said that he had, and he'd been keeping her in mind. "Nay, you only sought to be closer to the kitties. Do not lie to me."

"You are wrong, my dear. I did think of you. Often in a good way, but not always. You can be very vexing at times."

She laughed and he put out his hand for her. When she landed on his palm, he showed her what he needed. "I want this to be a reflection of the two of us. Not like in the olden days when it was velvets and dark, but something that we can come into and enjoy our time here before I rest. Do you understand? Oh, and please make a place for yourself. I should like for you to feel as welcome as I do when we are here."

"They are a very nice couple. And they have a wonderfully loving family. Well, he does. I so love Ollie. He is sad at times, but we have fun all the time when we are together." He agreed with her. "Do you think that they understand what we have done for them?"

"I have not told them." She looked at him. "When I saved her life, it wasn't my intention to make her like me, an immortal. But when I saw that she was mated to a grandson of my very good friend, I could not allow her to live on without him. They may not be as...understanding of that as I hope they will be."

"Because of the family." He nodded and sat down on a box that had been left behind. "You could do it for the rest of them, could you not? Make it so that we have them for eternity? I should like that, I think. I love them, Tanner."

"As do I. I could, but I don't know what they would think either. Ollie misses his mate very much. To do that to him would mean that he cannot join her. And while that has its advantages for the family as well, I do not think he'd be so happy. Then there are the others. To live a long time, Flora... you know as well as I that it can be lonely most of the time." She nodded. "We have been more than a little lucky in that we have each other, and have for some time. But Fredrick is gone, and my heart, it is pained."

"Yes, I miss him as well, and his humor. And you are correct in that living a long time is lonely. But it is boring too. You are very good company, but we see each other all the time. You are bored with life as well, I think." She looked so sad. "I will miss Fredrick for a very long time. He was the gentle side of you."

"Yes, we both will. But I'm afraid that we are needed here, for just a little while longer. At least until this mad man is under wraps. They have jailed the man, but he still has his men out there. I would like to see them destroyed before this is done." He wanted to end their conversation on a good note. "So, let us begin here. When you have decided what you would like, we'll do this together."

She moved around the room then, avoiding him so that he did not see her tears. But he could feel them, like daggers to his own heart. He loved the fae...she was his only friend besides Ollie. But he thought that the others, the great tigers, could be some as well, should he stay here.

He had lived a great many years. Most of them with Flora, but there had been others too. All, save the fae, had left him and Ollie behind. Ollie was a good man, never asking for anything in return for helping him all these years. The first time they'd met, Tanner had been staked to the ground in an open field.

"You need help?" It was barely dawn, the sun to blaze over him in a matter of minutes. "I'll help you, but you don't be biting me, all right?"

He made no such promises, not sure if he had it in him to do so. He'd been weak, his body cut and draining his life's blood onto the ground. But the man, Ollie, had seen his wounds and had wiped them clean with his own water jug, telling him he was sorry that men could be so cruel to another being.

When he was free, Ollie did the most incredible thing… he'd offered him his wrist, telling him that he was powerfully sorry that someone would have done this to him and wanted to make it right. From that moment on, they'd been friends, inseparable by only distance and time. But friends they had remained.

The room became theirs a few moments later. The magic that they shared would make things the way they wanted and bring in furniture from their home far from here. It was a place that he had been in a great deal until recently. Without Fredrick there, he doubted very much he'd return. It was good, he supposed, to be able to start anew. And with a better outlook.

Hurt beyond words no matter what he tried to tell his heart and mind, Tanner went to bed and closed his eyes. Flora said his name just as his body was beginning to shut down for the day.

"I should like to meet them." He told her to go ahead. "I should also like to work on the gardens at the other home. The one that is being written about. If you would allow it."

"The home belongs to Evan and his mate, Dylan. Tread carefully with her, she is as mean as a spider when crossed." She said she'd be careful. "And Flora, do not leave me. I don't mean today or when you need to go out, but I mean do not leave me alone for my lifetime. You are the only person, aside from my mate, that I love more than myself. I need you more than I've ever needed anyone, except Fredrick."

"I shall stay with you until you are dust, my lord. This I promise you." He nodded, his body going to sleep. "I love you, Tanner. Good day."

~~~

Flora finished his rooms, then set about making her own space. Tanner always gave her permission to have some space of her own, but she had never done it. Today, she thought that she might like to have it available. As she looked for the perfect spot, she felt the urge to be in the sunlight. Making sure that the magic was surrounding the entire house, she went outside.

There was much to see in this land. The trees were at their peak in color. In a few weeks the leaves would leave the limbs and fall to the earth, where other creatures would make use of them. Even the ground, in all its glory, would take some of the nutrients from them and use them as her own, giving back to the tree that blessed her with them. The circle of life was a wondrous thing.

The noise had her turning in all directions until she found the source. A man was cursing, and quite well too. Making her way to him, she was careful to figure out what he was before she made herself known to him. The man was a tiger, and he was very upset with the tractor he was near.

"Hello." He turned so suddenly that he nearly fell to the ground. But he was ready for her, if she were an enemy. His fists were doubled up and he was holding his body firmly, but she would cause him no harm. "I am Flora, fae to the vampire that lives here."

"Tanner." She smiled at him and he nodded. "I'm having some trouble today. My name is Adam, by the way. I don't suppose you know anything about tractors."

"Nay, I do not, but I can fix this for you." He asked her how. "I have my own magic. So long as you have no intentions of harming the ground nor the earth, I would gladly help you."

"I have to plow up the field here. Then I'm going to plant soy beans in it to be plowed under later in the spring. They're for the earth, vitamins and such for it. Does that count?" She said that it did. "I think that it's on his last legs. I might have to break down and buy a new one. I don't want to as this has been in our family for a great many years. But it's not running well, and hasn't been for some time."

"I don't understand you. Legs? It is but on wheels." He explained. "Ah, I see. But you would like for me to fix this one, yes?"

"If you can, I will be beholden to you. I have a lot of work to catch up on, and not much time." She nodded and touched the tractor. It was indeed old and tired. "Can you fix it?"

"I can, but we must strike a bargain, it's the way my magic works. I will do this, but what shall you give me in return?" Adam said that he understood. "Thank you."

"How about in the spring I plant you a field of wild flowers? An acre. That way, should you want, you can pick them or have them for a meal. My mom has been wanting a place to have flowers anyway." She was excited for such a treat. "You tell me which kind are your favorites, and I'll plant those as well."

"So many choices. I have heard that you can purchase seeds that have many varieties in them. Would that work?" He said it would be his pleasure. She touched her fingers to the great machine and healed it. The monster was like new, with the exception of the paint job. She might do that for him later as well. "The tractor will work now."

She had fixed it, thinking that her gift to him would be

something that she'd not want or use. But this, his gift to her, was very much needed for her simply because she loved flowers, of all kinds. And to have him say that he would plant her anything she wished was better still. She would have to ask Tanner for a catalog to look through. Or perhaps he could show her how to work the computer he used occasionally.

When the tractor started up, she smiled when Adam did. Then she asked him about the gardens at the other house, the one with the overgrown weeds in it. That was where she thought she could enjoy her days, a place where there was new growth and flowers in the ground.

"That's Evan and Dylan's. If you were to fix it up with me, I'd appreciate the help. I was going to start on it in the spring, after some of the shoots came up and I could tell what they were. I know a weed from a flower, and I love being outdoors, but until then, I don't know what they could be." She said she could do that now. "Well, as soon as I'm finished plowing, I'll meet you there. Would that be all right with you?"

She was so excited that she nearly forgot to go and check on Tanner. He was safe, and there was no one about, so she made her way to the other garden. Flora was going to enjoy staying here. There were so many places to help and have fun. Tanner would love it too once he was needed again.

Chapter 8

Madeline wasn't happy about her dress, but she was going to leave here soon and she was going to then see about her home. There wasn't any hope for those people going in and touching her things, but she knew they'd pay for cleanup. To think that they just went through her belongings like that.

She'd been arrested, again, and was in this stupid cell, again. This time for theft. Embezzlement, of all things. She'd not taken anything that would harm the country club or other places. And her husband's company could well afford it as well. It wasn't like it wasn't partly her money too.

Madeline had only just arrived at her home and the police had been waiting for her. She hadn't even been able to go inside...there were locks on her doors that she hadn't approved of. Not that she was able to complain about that either...they had cuffed her up and shoved her back into the stupid cruiser. Damned people were driving her crazy.

It was in here that she'd found out that her brother had died. Suicide. Why on earth would he do such a thing when she had it under control? And on top of that, now she had no access to the money that he promised to share with her when Alfred paid him. It was in some account that she'd not been given the information on. Samuel had really screwed the pooch on this one.

"Mrs. Richards? The van is here to take you to the funeral home." She stood up and then sat down. "Are you going? If not, then you should have told me before transport was made. We don't have time to cater to your every whim."

"Yes, I'm going. It is my brother's funeral, after all. But not in a van. There should be a limo, not a van. What were you thinking? You weren't, that's what. Go and tell the van to go away and get the limo ready." He opened the door and asked her to come with him. "So, there is a limo here. Don't be so stupid next time. I've had enough stressful things going on in my life without you trying to be humorous."

"I gave up trying to be nice or funny with you. It's wasted. There is a van. A police van that you'll be riding in, or you'll stay here. I don't know if you remember this or not, but you're a prisoner. And the only reason that you're getting out today is because your brother has passed away." She stared at the man. "You coming or not?"

"I can't be seen in a van, especially a police van." He started to shut the door. "I'm coming. Christ, this is the dumbest thing ever. My brother just had to go and hang himself right now. Did he not think what me going there in a police van was going to look like? Of all the dumb things he could have done. What about my things here? Who will pack them up?"

"Pack them up for what?" They were standing in a large open hall that had bars on each end. A woman, a police officer, came toward her with a set of chains. "You have to put these on now, and don't give me any crap, Mrs. Richards. If you do then I'm going to—"

"I am not wearing chains. How will I get around?" He said she'd be helped in and out of places. "Are you fucking kidding me? You expect me to wear chains on my arms like some sort of monster? I don't think so. This is getting out of hand, don't you think? Is this a power trip for you? Trying to make me look bad?"

"Look, lady, put them on or stay here. I have better things to do than to escort a woman that thinks the sun only shines for her. Wear the chains like you're supposed to, or go back to your cell. I don't really care." She glared at both of them, especially the woman, who laughed. "You can try that on me all you want, but I have four teenage boys that do it all the time. I'm immune to it. Now, chains or no chains. Either way, like I told you, it doesn't matter none to me."

In the end she wore the chains. Perhaps she could hide them with her shawl. But when they put them around her ankles too, she knew this just wasn't going to work. As she was opening her mouth to complain about how she'd look, the male officer told her to shut up.

"I don't want to hear how this isn't going to match your bag, nor about how it clashes with your shoes. Deal with it. If you didn't want to be here, wearing chains like the criminal that you are, then perhaps you should have thought things through better. Now, your sister is going to meet you there with her family. You'd be well off if you kept a civil tongue in your head and behaved. Or I swear to you, I'll bring you back here so fast that your head will wonder how that happened." She asked about her things. "What do you think you're going to do? Take them with you? They'll be here when you get back."

"I'm not coming back here. I have stuff to do. You'll have to pack them up for me. I have a house and family...well, my family has abandoned me, but I have a home that'll need to be taken care of after you people get done trashing it." She didn't say anything more, but Madeline knew that she was right. "Where is the funeral being held? I'm assuming that since Sunshine was in charge, it'll be all wrong. Christ, to think that Samuel did something so dumb and left it so Sunshine was in charge. Men. Can you believe they try so hard and fail so much?"

"My husband is an attorney, and a good one. So I'd appreciate it if you would keep the disparaging comments to yourself." Madeline doubted that and said as much. "You just go on believing that you're all that, and we'll see who comes out on top with this."

"If you say so." Madeline knew better. She was not only coming out on top, she was planning on suing the lot of them because of how they'd treated her. "And I will be leaving that place today. As I have said, I have much too much to do for me to be sitting around a cell all day."

The funeral home was one of the nicer ones in town. She'd asked around, just to see how she could make Sunshine feel badly for picking such a crappy place. Of course, she would have done better, no matter the venue. Sunshine wasn't that smart. Someone had to have helped her.

She wondered who was paying for this thing. She certainly wasn't. As she was taken from the van, her arms and legs in shackles, she asked when they were going to remove them. The policewoman told her they weren't and moved her along. How the hell was she supposed to do this?

"I demand that you remove this monstrosity from me. I don't know if you're aware of this or not, but I'm a big name around here. And people will wonder why I'm being treated so poorly. Remove them or be the laughingstock of this town." Again, she ignored her. "Did you hear me?"

"Everyone heard you, Maddie. You never did learn to use your inside voice, even as an adult." She looked at her sister. Had she not recognized the voice, she wouldn't have known it was Sunshine. Christ, she was beautiful. "Randal has come and gone with the girls. As you can well imagine, he doesn't want to have—"

"That won't work, Sunshine. Tell him to bring them back here. I don't care if he stays or not, but I won't be seen without my children. It's bad enough that I have to wear last year's clothing as well as these chains, but I won't be here in my hour of need all alone. Do you see what they've done to me?" Sunshine said that it was for her own good. "I decide what is for my own good. I suppose you expect me to pay for some of this. I'm not. And there is still the matter of paying for the girls' tuition to their camp. You've already incurred a late fee."

"I've taken care of our brother's arrangements. And I've told you, several times as a matter of fact, that I'm not paying anything for your children or Samuel's. Besides, I think that Randal has already enrolled them in public schools." Madeline would just see about that. "Are you ready to go in now?"

"I do not want to wear these things." The police officer just led her inside, right in front of everyone. But as soon as she got through the door to the funeral home, she could see that none of her friends were there anyway. "Did you put the notice in all the papers? Or did you skimp on that as well? I'm surprised that someone didn't come up to you and tell you what a piss poor job you've done with this, Sunshine. Samuel would be so ashamed of this mess."

It was beautiful. From the red rose spray that laid over his closed casket to the gorgeous arrangements around the room. She had no idea who they were from — her friends that simply couldn't make it, more than likely — but when she was escorted to the casket, she could see names on them that she didn't know. Whitfield. She didn't know any Whitfields, and asked her sister about them.

"They're my in-laws. I told you, I've gotten married to David. You should pay attention to what is said around you. But then, you're too busy finding fault with others to do that. As for the obit, no. I put it in the local paper. Doubtful that anyone would travel to see him anyway. You either." She glared at Sunshine and sat down when told. "This is going to be very short, and then we'll go to the cemetery. You can say a few words if you want."

"Am I going to be able to remove these chains to do so?" Sunshine said no. "Well, then I have nothing to say to any of you. Do whatever it is you're set up to do, but leave me out of it. And as I said before, don't expect me to pay for even a dime of this. But you will send me the planters. They'll be lovely in my home. You'd just kill them off. You were never any good at that sort of thing."

"No." She waited for Sunshine to say more. Like no to what? No she wasn't going to get them? No she wasn't a plant killer? Or no, she was going to pay for the funeral on her own? But the services began before she could get clarification.

The service was beautiful, despite Sunshine being in charge. There was music that she might have picked out herself, as well as the perfect tone to his life. Pictures were showing in the front of the room on a large screen, and she found herself remembering the days they were taken and smiling.

Samuel had been a great deal of fun over the years, and she was going to miss him. He'd been her only friend, as well as her partner in so many schemes. Just the thought of plotting and planning without him there to encourage her was sad to her.

When the service was over, Madeline stood with the rest of them, mostly David's family, and watched as mourners, not all that many, came to tell Sunshine that they were sorry for her loss. No one, it seemed, cared that she'd lost her only friend too. So she made sure that they did.

It really didn't take much for her to work up the tears. She would truly miss Samuel, but she was able to lay it on thick for a while. No one seemed to be paying attention to her, so she pretended to faint. That got people talking. It wasn't until she was being helped out by one of David's handsome brothers that she heard what others were saying.

"She's always been an attention grabber, even when things had nothing to do with her," she overheard someone say. Another said that she should have been jailed years ago. And one other group of catty women said she was responsible for Samuel's death, that she'd driven him to it. Before she could set them straight with her heel up their asses, she was shoved into the van again and buckled to the floor. The indignity was profoundly humiliating when the door was open while this was happening.

The place where her brother was being laid to rest was a pretty little spot, just under one of the larger trees that was in full color. Samuel so enjoyed the outdoors, and she knew that he'd have loved being right there. As the pastor talked about life and being a part of it, she watched her sister.

Sunshine had never been the type of woman to have men fawn all over her. She was more of the type that would be best friends to them and their companion on trips. But the man who stood next to her, he was attentive and supportive, holding her hand and then cradling her in his arms when she cried. No one had ever treated her with such tenderness, not that she could remember, and Madeline was sort of jealous of it.

Madeline was helped back into the van and she asked if there was a luncheon afterwards. The door slammed in her face as the officer that had come with her moved to the front of the vehicle. When she was in and buckled, Madeline asked again.

"For them? I would imagine so. For you, no. You're headed back to jail. And if you ask me once more why you're being returned there, I'm going to tape your mouth closed, and that'll be the end of it. Why can't you just be a quiet depressed woman like normal people? Or are you inhuman about everyone and everything but how it affects you?" She knew that she'd not allow her to do that, so she asked anyway. It thrilled her to irritate the woman cop. "Talk to your attorney. He'll have the scoop for you when you get there. That is if you still have questions. Wait, what am I talking about? You always have questions, even if it's laid out for you in perfect answers."

She didn't even understand why she was in the jail in the first place. The only thing that she'd gotten was that her credit cards and bank accounts were seized and that her husband had left her. Randal wasn't all that much of a loss. She'd only kept him around for appearances, and of course the nice job that he had. But as far as being much in the way of a helpmate, he'd never been all that much of one.

Oh, he would try. But she'd end up having to redo his mess. Even getting the kids ready for school when she was away. She'd been so ashamed that he wouldn't make sure that their clothing was ironed just perfectly nor their hair done. What did he think was going to happen to them when they got there? They'd be the joke of the week. She would not allow that to happen.

The attorney was waiting for her when she returned. It wasn't the one from the firm that she and Randal had used before, but a court appointed one. She asked him why he was there and not someone with a real degree.

"I have a real degree, Mrs. Richards. I graduated from Harvard at the top of my class. I would like to talk to you about your case. There are a few things that we need to discuss for when you're in the courtroom." She asked him who was paying him. "My firm does pro-bono cases several times a month. You just happened to come up when it was my turn. Now, about your case?"

"Why am I here?" He asked her if she remembered her rights. "I do, but I don't know why I was given them, nor why someone thought it was a good idea to bring me here. I'm sure that it's nothing more than a misunderstanding. Or a ploy to get me into trouble with people. Is my sister doing this? It would be like her to make me look bad."

"You were arrested for several things, as a matter of fact. Misappropriation of company funds from your husband's company. Embezzlement from the county club where you were treasurer. The children's school is saying that you owe over ten thousand dollars in back fees and payments for their tuition." She waited for more while he read over the paper. Not that she believed there to be that much, but he looked like he was searching for it. "It also says that you were part of the attempted murder of your sister."

"She would be dead by now had I been a part of his plan. So that's not going to stick. Anyone who knows me is aware that when I'm in charge of something, it gets done, no matter what I have to do." She didn't mind admitting this to him. There were rules that he had to abide by. "Samuel told me that he had killed her. He fucked that up too, as you can see. As for the tuition and fees, Sunshine was supposed to pay those bills. She was sent them a long time ago. The rest? I just took a little here and there. Not enough for anyone to be upset over."

"They *are* upset, a great many people to be honest, and they want it all back. It looks as if you took nearly a hundred thousand from the country club, and nearly that much from the firm your husband works for. Saying that you only took a little here and there isn't going to cut it when you go to court." She didn't think he had that right and told him. "They even have you on camera taking it, Mrs. Richards. I would like to propose that you plead guilty to the charges if I can get them to reduce time for you. That way, instead of staying in jail for ten years for each count, you can serve both for ten. As for the charges against you about attempted murder, I'm afraid that's going to be harder to get reduced. There is enough evidence on that to get you the death penalty. If they want to go that far."

"You aren't saying I'm going to have to stay here, are

you?" He shook his head. "Well that's good. Christ, I want to go home. There is no telling what sort of mess I have there. As for killing off Sunshine, I had nothing to do with it. I knew that he was going to do it, he told me, but I wasn't there. I want you to take that off the list of things that they're going to try and blame on me. And another thing, I would like for you to get me some nicer clothing. This orange thing is not suited to my lifestyle."

"Wait a moment. Are you saying that Samuel told you he was going to kill Sunshine? And you did nothing to stop him? You are aware that knowing and not doing anything is almost as bad as pulling the trigger, don't you?" She shrugged. "She's your sister. Doesn't that mean anything?"

"No. I have never cared for her anyway. And there was a big pay off when she was dead. Samuel got some of the money. I mean, he was going to split it with me. Which reminds me, I'd like for you to see about getting it for me. He's not going to use it, is he? It would have been a good deal of money. But now that I think on it, I never saw any of it." He asked her where the money was supposed to come from. "Alfred James. Sunshine was into his business, doing some things that got him closed down. He wanted her to pay, and I had no problem with it either. I mean, she should mind her own business."

He just sat there, his face unreadable. When he stood up and told her she was going to have to get someone else, Madeline asked him why.

"Because you conspired to kill your own sister, and was going to take money, blood money, to do so. You ripped off the companies you worked with by nearly half a million dollars, and all you can think about is getting money and going home. I can't represent you." He was at the door when he turned back to her. "Good luck with your next attorney, Mrs. Richards. I think you're going to need it."

She had no idea what she was supposed to do now. So when someone came to get her, to take her back to her little cell, Madeline didn't even argue about the clothing this time. Right now she had bigger things to worry about. Like where the fuck was her money? Things were not going well, she realized, and she had no idea how to fix it.

Well, she supposed someone would have to. Next time she saw Sunshine, she'd have to tell her she needed a better attorney. No more of this free shit would work. Laying down, she smiled. She'd be home soon, she knew it.

~~~

David looked up when he saw a movement out of the corner of his eye. He'd been working since they'd gotten back from the thing at Evan's home. David asked Sunny if she was all right.

"Yes, I was just looking around the house. Did you know that there isn't a single television here?" He said he didn't watch much television, but they could get one. "No, that's not necessary. I was just saying that there wasn't one. Also, and this is strange, the plants that you have here, inside and out, are twice the size they were this morning. I know why now, but I had no idea why when I noticed it."

"The fae, Flora, I think her name is." She said it was. "She's also helping Adam at Evan's house. She loves flowers. And she knows what they are before they bloom. She told him that she would work with him. Also, she fixed the tractor, and it works better now than it did when we first started using it after Dad retired."

"Yes, so I heard. She told me that she didn't think ours were doing so well, so she gave them a little boost. I had no idea what that might have entailed, but they do look better. Especially the herbs in the kitchen. Speaking of which, I'm making rosemary chicken with baked potatoes for dinner, if you're hungry." He told her that he was. "And I guess we're going to have fruit in the summer. She's done something to the ones you have here too. I think she mentioned cherries and apples."

"That sounds amazing. What is really wrong?" She just sat there and he leaned back to wait. "When you have time, would you look through the trunk that was found in the attic of the house? There are some things in there that you might like to add to your collection of teapots. They're—"

"I've touched a few things in their home. Nothing on purpose, but there are some things that are in there that I had to. Doorknobs and such. Anyway, I touched a picture frame, just to straighten it up a little. It has a lot of stories to it. I asked Dylan about it, and she said they found it in a room upstairs." He asked her what she'd felt. "It's had a lot of pictures in it, the frame I mean. And one being the cardboard that was holding the current photo in it. It's been there the longest, along with the glass that holds the pictures."

"Did you tell Dylan or Evan?" She shook her head. "Is it bad? I mean, this thing you're trying very hard not to tell me, is it bad?"

"Not bad, no. At least I don't think so. It's a map of the underground path that people had to take." That didn't sound like much. "And where the money and other things that they might need along the way are hidden. There is a lot of it too. Or so the person who put it in there thought. I don't know the value compared to today's prices, but there is some."

"How many stops along the path, do you know?" Sunny said she didn't know, only that it was littered with things to pick up. "That sounds like clothing and food too. I mean, that would, of course, be rotted, but to find something that it would have been hidden in there would be great."

"Coin, is what he thought of it as. I don't know about paper money. But yes, there was clothing too. I guess we need to tell them, let them find out what it is." He nodded. "I don't want them to think I was snooping around. I was only just marveling at the frame. It's very stunning. It looks like something that you'd find in a high classed auction house. And while it was a little off, it wasn't bad enough that I *had* to touch it."

"They'd never think that. And once you tell them what you discovered, they'll be so excited that it's doubtful they'd think of anything else." She didn't seem convinced. "Come on, let's go tell them. It'll be fun to see the look on their faces when you show it to them. And who knows about the money? It'll be like a treasure hunt for us."

"You're sure?" He said he was positive and told her that they'd be happy. "I like them both, all your family actually, and I don't want them to think I'm a freak."

"We're cats living in a world of humans that can change with a thought. We have a vampire living in our basement with a tiny fae. I think that if anyone thought you were that, they'd have to deal with us too. But they won't. It'll be good."

He was going to talk to Evan before they got there to warn him that she was afraid to tell them, but he knew his brother would be grateful for any news about the house.

David

Chapter 9

Alfred waited on his new attorney in the meeting room. The man was supposed to be bringing him not just a phone that he could use, but also some cash. Money talked, and as soon as he could speak the language of the people around there, he'd be getting things done. So far all he'd managed in there was zip. And he wanted answers too.

Like why was he not getting the information on Sunshine that he wanted? He knew she was still alive…the paper had talked of nothing else but her since her brother had killed himself. And that was another thing. Had Sam given them more information than he should have? If so, he wanted someone out there that could deal with his family. Just because he was dead didn't mean they should be alive. Fuck that crap. He wanted them to pay too.

When the man showed up, he knew that he wasn't going to be any help at all. He was one of those stick men, he liked to call them. Stick to the rules. Stick to the way things go normally. And worse yet, a stick up his ass. Alfred was sure he had a stick name, too. More than likely something like Peter Farthing. He decided to call him Fart. If he did say his real name, Alfred had no idea what it was. When he sat down and asked how he was doing, Alfred told him he was being fucked up the ass.

"You are?" He said that he wasn't, but was making sure he was paying attention. "I assure you, Mr. James, I pay attention to everything. I'm to understand that your last lawyer, Mr. Michaels, met with an accident."

"You could say that." Alfred had been visited by the pack alpha a few days after he'd been brought here. Not only was he being blamed for the man's death, but apparently he had to pay a fine too. Like he had that sort of money just laying around in his cell. "I was hoping for some extras, like a phone and computer. I have a business to run, and it's not going to be there when I leave here if I can't at least talk to my foreman."

He had no foreman. He didn't even have a secretary any longer. When they'd gone into his company a few months ago, everyone there had not only been arrested, but had been offered some deals too. Alfred had no idea if they had talked yet, but they'd better run and hide if they did. He told them when he hired them that saying a word to the cops would get them dead.

"Yes, well, that's not going to be possible. I've heard that you had those items before and it hadn't been approved. I believe that someone is still going over some of the information that was on them. Bad move, I'm afraid. That's a sure way to get caught up in the judicial system. Getting them for you now will be impossible." Figures. He'd have to think of another way to get them. "There is a bargain on the table. If you were to tell them where the other lab is, as well as whatever monies you have stashed away, it could cut a great deal off your sentence. Such as the death penalty. And from what I'm to understand, they're going for that instead of life. You'd be better off telling someone everything you have."

"You just want me to tell them everything there is about me and my businesses? Like that's going to help me? I don't know if you realize this or not, but I'm not really a good guy. And I can tell you that because I know for sure that you can't use that against me." He said nothing. "Also, me telling you everything? Well, I'm reasonably sure you don't want to know it all so you can sleep at night."

The man just sat there, his face as unreadable as any he'd ever witnessed before. It made him slightly uncomfortable to be stared at so intently. But when Fart spoke again, Alfred didn't know what to think.

"You might think that you're all bad ass, Mr. James, but I assure you that you're not even a drop in the ocean that goes on around you. As for your illicit ideas that things you might tell me would give me nightmares, I assure you, I'm made of sterner stuff. Now, if we're going to be here together, I'd like to know everything. I do not want to be blindsided by something that comes to me in the courtroom that I don't already have an answer for. And I'm going to record this so that I don't miss anything later when I go over my notes. What sort of businesses do you run?"

What the fuck, he decided. "I run a lab, or used to, that dealt in making new drugs for different companies. At least that's what it looked like to the public. But what we really did was make synthetic drugs for getting doped up. Mostly for the high living customer, as things are expensive. Gotta love the American dream. Also, as a way to test these drugs, I have this lab in an underground facility that uses, for the most part, the homeless and the underbelly of the world. That is where the real money is." He asked him if he had access to it. "The money? Not from in here, not without my computer. The lab, yes. It's only a few steps from the lab that is legit."

"I see. And do you visit this other lab often?" He asked him why that would matter. "Well, it would go, I imagine, a long way in someone saying that you did it all when you could say, maybe, that you didn't know it was there. Establishing facts about it, you could say."

"I knew it was there. It was all my idea. All the way down to how the fucker looked when it was done. When I was in college, I took some drafting classes. Did really well in them, and that helped me when it came time to build it. No, I did it all on my own." The man wrote down everything which seemed silly to him, since he was recording it too. "What are you going to do with all this? Can you get me out of here?"

"Most assuredly, you'll be leaving here, and soon. We just have to clear some things up and get this trial finished up." He thought that was great and said as much. "There are some other things we need clarified. Did you or did you not pay Samuel Davis to kill Sunshine Davis? There are reports that you gave him a large sum of money, with the promise of paying him more over the next several years."

"Yeah, I paid him. Fat lot of good it did me. He was supposed to make her dead, not running around making my life more difficult. As for the sums...I paid him three million for the hit, then I was to give him a million for the next five years on the anniversary date of her death. Sort of in celebration. He's dead, I heard. To be honest, I'm glad. Now I won't have to pay him anything, nor that other sister."

David

"Yes, Mr. Davis hung himself when it was apparent that he was going to jail. And Mrs. Richards? The sister to Sunshine and Samuel, was she aware of this transaction?" He said that she was the one that brokered the deal that Samuel got money for the next several years. "Their spouses? Of either of them? Did they know?"

"No. It was supposed to be this big windfall for the two of them. Both of them was gonna go away or something. There is this.... What does this have to do with me getting out of here?" He told him. "Okay, I can see that. Giving you enough to hang them too is a good idea. I guess having me turn on them is an added bonus for me. I'm sure that the men in the big offices, they want them too. Shame that Sunny had to live though. Just think of how many other businesses she's going to ruin by being out there. Anyway, yeah, the sister knew. That Madeline, she's a piece of work. She tried to get twice the amount that Sam and I agreed on so that she could have a bigger cut too. I don't have any family, but seeing them all together conspiring against their own blood...well, that scared me a bit."

They talked for another hour. It was nice, he thought, having an attorney that he could unload on, sort of brag about himself. With Ralph, since he'd known everything there was to know about him, hell, even being a part of it, Alfred had never realized how boring it had been. He did lie a little on some of the things he'd done. Not what he'd done, but he'd not been the one that came up with some of the ideas he'd had. And since no one was here to say otherwise, he'd had a blast with it. When their time was done, Alfred hated to see him leaving.

"You will see me in the courtroom. I'll make sure that

you have a nice suit and tie. There will also be something for you to have for dinner. Sort of your last meal here after this is done. And for the love of all that is holy, don't talk to anyone else. You do and you'll fuck this up for us both." He promised him that he'd not do that. "Good. All right, I have to get my notes together. I'll see you tomorrow."

After he left, Alfred didn't mind going to his cell. It would be the last time he'd be in here, he knew it. That man was going to make things happen. He might even pay him a big fat bonus when this was done and just give him the money meant for Sam. And he was going to see about getting Fart put on his payroll. It would do him good to have someone on his side for a change instead of having to bribe Ralph all the time.

Fart did have a suit delivered before bedtime, and a meal fit for a king. Steak that was an inch thick. A potato so big that he hadn't been able to finish it off with the bacon bits, the real kind, sour cream, and butter. There was even a loaf of hot bread with more butter, and a huge slice of cake that he savored each bite of. Yes, sir, he thought to himself, he was going to bring Fart on if it was the last thing he did.

~~~

Adrian felt dirty, like his body was covered in the same filth that was on Alfred. He'd felt worse last night when he'd gotten home, but today, it was like he'd been bathed in slime and evilness. As he sat with his family, as far in the back as possible, he had to smile. This was the best thing he'd ever done, and he was glad that he'd been a part of it. As soon as the courtroom was called to order, he stood with the others while the judge had a seat.

The prisoner, Alfred James, was brought in then. The new

suit looked good on the man if he did say so himself. And if he had a self-satisfied expression on his face, well, that would soon change too. Alfred asked the man next to him at the table who he was.

The argument got louder and louder as they sat there. It was funny, really. His entire family was trying their best to listen to it while holding onto their mirth. The only person who didn't think it was funny was the judge. He looked pissed.

"Is there a problem?" Alfred stood up and said that he needed his attorney. "That is your attorney, Mr. James. He was assigned to you a few days ago by me. Your previous one has, sadly, passed away."

"I know that. I was told all about it, and charged a fine too. But this isn't the man that I saw last night. The one that took all those notes. I'd like to have him here." He asked his name. "Well, I really didn't pay any attention to that. I was calling him Fart in my head. I figured that he had a name like that, Farthing. Or something. Anyway, we talked and he said I was going to get out of jail for good."

"So a man you don't know came to see you and you didn't ask his name? I don't suppose you ever caught the firm's name when he came in?" Alfred said that he hadn't. "Did you sign a contract? Get a business card?"

"No. I thought he'd be here today." The judge leaned over to his bailiff and spoke quietly to him. "I was sent this suit and a wonderful dinner to celebrate. I don't know what's going on."

The judge let him ramble on, and Alfred was doing a good job of it then stopped. Adrian hoped Alfred realized what he'd done, but to be sure, he'd have to ask him. The man just seemed to shut down.

"The only visitor you had last night was Adrian Whitfield. You did have Mr. Parker come, but you turned him away. That's the man there that you're sitting next to." The judge looked in Adrian's direction and he stood up. "Did you see this man last night?"

"Yes, sir, I did." Alfred stood up and turned to look at Adrian. He knew then…the man knew what he'd just done. "We had a long talk about why he was in jail. And for the record, Your Honor, I never told him my name. He didn't ask."

"You told me you were an attorney." Adrian said that he never once said that he was. "You told me I'd be getting out of jail. What the fuck were you doing there if not as my attorney?"

"You assumed you knew who I was. I just never corrected you. And as for you getting out of jail, I never said that either. I said that with what you told me, you'd be leaving the jail you were currently in. You're going to prison, I hope." The courtroom burst into laughter, but Adrian didn't join in. "I have the information that Mr. James willingly shared with me, Your Honor. I have only shared this with my sister-in-law, Dylan Whitfield, and she has shared it with her boss."

"And who the hell might that be?" Before he could answer, if he was inclined to do so, Dylan stood up. "What the hell are you doing here?"

Instead of answering, she asked for and got permission to step up to the dais. There was some major shit about to happen, and when the judge said this would be finished in his offices, the police stood in front of the door leading out and Adrian was escorted to the backroom. Henry Cobb was sitting in one of the chairs waiting on them.

"Hello, Harold. It's been a long time." Harold Courtright sat down in his chair after shaking hands with Henry. "I've been helping out with this case. Behind the scenes, so to speak, but you have enough now to get this piece of slime off the streets. I wanted to make sure that you didn't need anything else, or see if you had any questions for us. I have to tell you, Harold, it's been a horrific battle with this one."

"Thank you. I'm certain with what you were able to gather was all done legally. But I have to ask, what makes this important to you? I should know, don't you think?" Henry pointed at Adrian. "You're helping him get his running ticket in a better position? I don't believe that any more than I think that man out there is innocent of all charges like he said."

"Adrian is going to take my job one day soon and I want to help him. Besides, you know Dylan and her family. She's my girl." There was just enough hardness in his voice to indicate that there was no more information forthcoming about either of them. "Adrian did a good job in talking to Alfred. I've listened to the tapes, and there is also video of the conversation. That might not be admissible in court, but the recordings will be. He confessed to everything. And the lab that he talks about that he runs has been shut down as well. A great many people will be thrilled with that."

"For you and your boy here." He didn't sound upset any longer, just resigned. "I don't want to sound like a bastard here...I'm happy as hell that this is done. But I'm up for reelection soon myself, and I'd like to come away with something here. Henry, you know as well as I do that the younger and better looking the judge, the more votes he can get. What can I say about this that'll not get me in trouble when our boy here runs on his own ticket?"

"This is all for you, Harold, if you play ball my way. You'll say that you listened to the tapes, had a man go and check them out, and now you've closed it down, with the help of Adrian." A file was put in front of Harold. "That has your name all over it. The warrant is there, as well as the arrest record of each of the men working there. You'll also find that I will send you a letter of commendation; it'll be coming in the mail soon."

The judge looked things over and then glanced at Adrian. He was sure he had questions, a great many of them, but all he did was thank him. Adrian sat down then, his legs just giving out on him.

"This lab, it's gone?" Henry said that it was being taken care of as they sat there talking. "Do I need to know how?"

"No, and neither does the public. Suffice it to say that no one will be able to get inside it, nor will they ever be able to use it again. It's gone." Adrian didn't even look at Dylan. She had made sure that everything the president said was true. Henry stood up and put out his hand. "Harold, you have some good people working for you in this town. I'd use them more if I were you. Think of all the goodwill the people will have for you."

"I think I'll take you up on that." Harold sat down after the president left and looked at Adrian and Dylan. "You all right with what has happened in here today? I don't mean the president coming here—nice touch, by the way—but with the proceedings as he said them? Me taking credit?"

"We're more than okay with it. It was Adrian's idea to do this, as well as to have Henry come here and talk to you." Again, Adrian said nothing. All lies, but he could live with it. "Also, you should know that if you ever need anything, and I do mean anything, you let me know. I have more than enough people I can call on to get most things done. You're a good man, judge, and I can work with that. How about you working with me?"

"If you get results like this, yes, I'd be honored to work with you. I believe in you. And thank you for this."

As they were leaving his office, to give him time to go over things, Adrian asked her about the lie.

"You're going to need him more than he'll realize. Also, and you might not have thought of this, but your business is going to boom. My advice to you is, close it down now. Before it gets out of hand." He asked her how she'd come up with that. "People are going to see you as the next fucking big thing. The man who can find shit and get it done. You will be working all the time and not getting shit done that you need to. Like running for governor. Close it down now, and open it in about a month as a campaign office. I think Lily will love you for it."

It was moving too fast. Not the governor's job, but everything else. Like he was on a runaway train he couldn't get off of. Leaning against the wall for a moment, he thought about being governor and then hopefully president. He'd need a plan. Not only that, but he'd need people working for him, other than family, that could get him there. And he needed to start on that now.

He called Lily while he was standing in the hallway. She was thrilled to know that things had worked out for them, and that the office wouldn't be open for much longer. She, like Dylan, had a feeling that it was going to be hectic now that his name was being attached to bigger and better things. Lily told him that she'd gotten some strange calls since yesterday.

"Like from who?" She told him. "How the hell did it already come out in the paper that I helped here? Christ, there must be someone recording this shit." She said it was an unknown source, but she thought it was one of the cops that had been there. "More than likely. So close us down, turn off the phone, and take a month vacation with pay. Enjoy."

"You can count on it. And when this is done, you call me and I'll run you the best campaign you've ever seen. All right?" Adrian said it was a deal. "Great. You have fun, and don't find a mate until I get back. You never know, she might not like me."

"Then she's out the door. Anyone that doesn't care for my best employee, then they're not going to be good enough for me." They both laughed and Adrian felt good. Going into the courtroom to hear what was going to happen to James, he sat down with a smile. This was going to be impressive.

Chapter 10

Sunny woke with her back being massaged. Well, her body was, but it was her back that she noticed first. As nails dug into her flesh, she lifted her head enough to see not only were there huge paws on her, but a large tiger as well. He licked her face when she smiled at him.

"I don't know if you are aware of this or not, but that isn't all that sexy. Your tongue is rough and your teeth are scary sharp that close to my eyes." The cat on her purred. "David, what are you doing?"

You were so upset last night that I know you didn't sleep well. And this morning, he wanted you so badly, but I convinced him that you needed to rest. Making you relax seemed a smart move. She laid back down and felt the way he pushed his paws carefully into her shoulders. *If you were to roll over, he'd love to have a taste of you. I bet you're all dewy in the morning.*

Moving from her belly, the big cat sat on the floor. Almost as soon as she was on her back, he joined her in the bed again. Spreading her legs for him, she cried out the moment his mouth touched her hot pussy.

He was the best at this. Of course she didn't know any other cats, so of course he was the best for her, but she enjoyed his mouth on her. And when he began fucking her with his big knobby tongue, she came three more times. But he didn't seem to be finished with her just yet. As soon as he licked her thigh, she heard David saying no in her mind. But it was too late by then. The tiger bit down on her leg hard enough to break bones.

Sweat beaded on her flesh she hurt so much. And when he shook his great head, she cried out and lost consciousness. Waking not more than a few seconds later, the cat was just pulling his mouth from her leg.

The pain was hard to breathe around. Not only that, but she felt weak with it...her body burned now. And when she felt David's pain too, like he was worried for her and felt hers, she had to concentrate very hard on what he was saying.

He's changing you. She vaguely remembered asking him into what, but the cat bit her again, this time in the fleshy part of her belly. The pain was compounded by him tearing at her harshly.

Holding onto her stomach contents was impossible, and Sunny knew that she had thrown up everywhere. Even as she lay there, smelling of death and vomit, she knew that she wasn't going to make it. That she was as dead as she had been before. Only this time, she loved the person who had done it to her.

How could anything as beautiful as sex with her mate turn into something like this? she wondered as the light seemed to be swallowed up by death. As her body began to float away, so did her thoughts of ever having a wonderful life with David.

There were noises where she was. Death wasn't quiet harps and music, Sunny thought. When she saw her mom and dad, she almost didn't know them. They were dressed as she remembered them being all the time…soft pants and T-shirts, like they had only just come in from the surf and were trying to relax. Her mom spoke to her first.

"I don't think you're supposed to be here, darling." Her heart broke. She'd not be able to spend time with her parents? What sort of cruelty was this? "You go on back there now. David is such a wonderful person."

"David Whitfield?" She looked at the other woman sitting next to her parents and nodded. "Oh my goodness, Ollie must be so happy right now. And you expecting and all."

"Expecting what?" They all thought that was funny, and Sunny wished she understood what they were talking about. "I died. His cat, David's cat, was changing me and I died."

"No, child…not all dead, that is." She shook her head. "You've been here before. Remember? Well, perhaps not. But this time you will." The woman sat down beside her as the room she was in shifted and filled up. "Here, have a cookie. I love them so much. White chocolate chip with macadamia nuts are my favorite. How about yours?"

"I like raisin nut. Where am I if I'm not all the way dead? I don't even know what that means." She was handed a cookie, and wasn't the least bit surprised that it was a raisin nut. "Where am I?"

"I'm not sure I know how to explain that. I'm Rose, Rose Whitfield, mate to Ollie. I died some time back. Doesn't seem so long ago, but it has been. How is he?" She told her that he was grieving, but doing okay. "Oh good. I was so afraid that he'd want to join me. He can't, you know. Join me. He has to stay for the new babies that are coming. And to tell me all about them."

"I have no idea what you're talking about." She laughed again. "Okay, so you can't tell me where I am. You know Ollie, who is a sweetheart, by the way, and also you know David, who is my mate. I'm so confused. Is death going to be like this all the time?"

"I don't think so. But you're not dead, I told you that." So she had. Sunny asked her what she meant about babies. "Oh, well, you're going to have one. And that wonderful girl that Ollie tells me about, Dylan, she and my grandson, Evan, are going to adopt two soon as well. I don't think they're aware of it just yet, however."

"I think if I were going to adopt children, I'd know about it. I'm not sure about anything much right now, but I'd remember that part if I had children coming. Don't you think?" She smiled at her. "What can you tell me, if not the other things?"

"Well, I want you to know that you're going to make a wonderful tiger. And not to be too harsh on my David when you wake up." Sunny asked if she was going to wake. "Oh yes. You're an immortal, my dear. Tanner did that to you when he saved your life. And since he didn't want to have you here when something happened to David, he too is immortal. The rest are not. Not yet at any rate. But I do have a favor to ask of you. When you go back, and you will soon, will you please tell my Ollie that I think of him daily, and that if I see him here before his time, I'm going to be very cross with him. Also, please tell him that I love him with all my heart. And even though it doesn't beat any longer, it will forever be his. You tell him that."

"I will. And that's perhaps the most beautiful thing I've ever heard." Rose thanked her. "My family doesn't say those sorts of things to each other. And my brother, Samuel, he's gone."

"Yes, sad thing that was. It took your parents several days to get over that one. But he's resting now. In his own place. Watch out for that sister, however. She's not one to be trusted, no matter what she says." Sunny said she knew that. "Good. All right then, it's time for you to go. You've been here much too long as it is. You'll tell them that I love them, won't you, Sunshine? Tell them that I want them to carry on and be a family."

Breath filled her as she sat up in the bed. David was there, his head bent over her body, and he was crying. Touching her fingers to his forehead, he sobbed loudly before grabbing her up into his arms and holding her. Wrapping her arms around him, she told him how much she loved him and asked him if he was all right.

"Yes, fine now that you're here. Christ, I have never been so terrified in all my life. You were.... I couldn't hear your heart beating, and I knew that I'd killed you. I'm so sorry, Sunny. With all my heart and soul, I'm so terribly sorry that I did this to you." She told him she was fine. "He killed you. Again. I don't know what came over him, but he just did this without my permission."

"I saw your grandma." That stopped him, and he told her that she was gone, that she had died. "Yes, I was talking to her. She said that—"

"She said what?" David was looking at her strangely, and then he told her to lie back. "You rest, and when you feel better, we'll talk about this dream you—"

"She loved white chocolate chip cookies with macadamia nuts in them. She has the greenest eyes I've ever seen, and she is beautiful. Her name is Rose." He nodded. "She told me that we're going to have a baby. And that Evan and Dylan are going to adopt two children soon. She didn't say when, but I had a feeling that she might not know."

"You spoke to my grandmother and she told you we were going to have a baby." She didn't care for his tone and told him that. "Honey, I think I just killed you, and now you're telling me that you spoke to my dead grandmother."

"She had a message for your grandfather too." He asked her what that might be. "She told me to tell him that even though her heart no longer beats, that it will forever be his."

For some reason that got his attention. And when he asked her about the visit, this time he was much more believing. Sunny asked him what had changed his mind.

"When my grandma was alive, she used to tell us that someday we'd find our other halves, and that even after our hearts would stop someday, it would forever belong to our other halves." He stood up, pulling on clothing. "We have to go."

"Where?" He threw clothing at her, and when he hit her with a shoe, she told him to stop a moment and answer her. "Where are we going?"

"To see Evan. He'll run a test and confirm what we already know." He picked her up and swung her around the room. "We're going to have a baby. A baby, can you believe it?"

She did, but didn't think that now was the time to tell him that they were going to live forever. Sunny didn't want to freak him out again. So she got dressed, smiling the entire time, knowing that she was going to be the best mom that she could be. Not counting Eve.

~~~

Ollie had her repeat it several times. His Rose, the love of his life, was talking to him. Not really, but it was as close as he could get to it without joining her. And the news of the baby? Well, that had him in all kinds of feels.

"She said that if I joined her before my time, I'd be in trouble with her?" Sunny said that she had. "I don't suppose when she said that would be, did she? I have to tell you, darling, I miss her terribly."

"Yes, well, she told me to tell you that you have to come and tell her about the new babies. She's enjoyed the stories that you told her about myself and Dylan." Yes, he'd been going to see her for some time now, every day when he could get there. There were times when he'd not say a word, just go and sit with her. "Ollie, she is the most beautiful woman I've ever seen. And she gave me cookies."

"Yes, she loved cookies. Her one downfall, she always told me. I'd buy them for her, hiding them around the house like they were for me, but to be honest, I never cared for them like she did. It gave me the most pleasure just to see that she'd been into the stash of them. My Rose, she'd not make a pig of herself, just eating one or two, but I'd know." Sunny kissed him on the head and he held her to him, gently. "I'm so glad that you got to know her, even for that little time there. She was my greatest joy."

"And you were hers too, Ollie." He nodded, his heart just too full for words. "Can I tell you something else? She said that Evan and Dylan were going to adopt two children. While she didn't tell me when, I got the feeling that it was soon. Rose wanted you to tell her all about the new babies too."

"Really?" She nodded. "Oh my child, I have to tell you something too. I just heard from Evan that there are a couple of young boys that need a home. They're a mite on the big side — one of them is fourteen, the other about ten — but they're going to help find them a home. You think it could be them?"

"She didn't say how old they'd be, only that they'd be adopting them." He wanted to ask Evan about it, but he was sworn to secrecy. He did so love the idea about having some kids around that he could talk to, but babies were sure nice too. "I'll not say a word until they do."

Sunny thanked him and walked away. Ollie just sat there, his mind working a million miles a minute. And when dinner was called, he nearly didn't hear them leaving him. All he could think about was Sunny bringing him a message. Then something else occurred to him. He went to the dining room to look into it.

"You're a tiger." David laughed and he felt his face heat up. "What I meant to say was, congratulations on being a tiger. You sure did get up and around pretty quick. I thought humans were down for a few days, if not longer."

"Perhaps I had a message or two to bring back, and that got me healed faster." Yeah, Ollie could see that, but he had a feeling that wasn't all it was. He looked up when Tanner joined them.

"You did this." He said that he had not, but he might have helped a little. "Yeah, I thought so. The blood you gave her, that helped her out a little more than usual. I'm not complaining, my friend, but I am glad that you're here all the time. It's nice having someone from my past, even if he does look like he's younger than my son."

"Thank you, I think. And yes, it was the blood I gave her the first time I was with her. And so you know, Flora had a little to do with it as well. She's fallen hard for your family, Ollie." He said that he had for her as well. "I'm staying here, for a while. David and his mate have given me permission to stay in their lower levels. It suits me."

"You could have come and stayed with me in the big house." He said that there was much too much going on around David at the moment. "That woman and man. I understand that. They're a little on the mean side. And they sure do have it bad for my Sunshine. You gonna help them out? Keep them safe for us?"

"Yes. The man is on his way to a prison that will hold him for a long time. The woman, she'll be trouble yet. I have seen it." Ollie had forgotten that Tanner could see a little into the future. "The woman, she will be dealt with. I don't know how it happens. Just that her life is ended. And Sunshine is safe from her."

"She gonna hurt anyone in this family while she's about her stuff?" He said that she'd never get the chance as far as he'd seen. "You see that she doesn't. I got me some great grandbabies and kids coming, and I don't want that messed up. Nor do I want you hurting either. I think you've suffered enough by those people."

"I thank you, my friend, and you don't need to worry about the babies, large ones or small. Ever. And I shall have to make myself honorary uncle to them. What do you think the boys would say to that?" Ollie wasn't sure if he was kidding or not, and told him they'd love him as much as the rest of them did. "Yes, a queer old vampire that is alone for the most part."

"You want me to kick your ass?" Tanner just looked at him. "You thinking that because I'm an old man I can't do that? If I can't, I sure do know someone that can. You don't dare talk about that anymore. You're as much a part of this family as my son and grandsons. You hear me? Why, I love you. And even though you're a bloodsucker, I don't care about the rest. You're a good man, Tanner. No matter the other stuff."

The room had grown quiet, and he looked around. They were staring at him and Tanner like they'd missed something. When he started to tell them what the old vamp had said, Dylan got up and came to their side of the table. He wasn't sure what she was planning, but he didn't want her hurting him.

"You are the best person in the world, have I ever told you that?" He said that they were all remiss in telling him that, so no. "Well, we will from now on. You have a heart of gold, and a good head on your shoulders too. I'm proud to call you my grandda."

"Not that I don't appreciate this compliment, but what brought that on? You don't strike me much as the mushy type. And if you're trying to butter me up for something, honey, all you have to do is ask and it's yours." They laughed again and he wanted to snap at them, but he held his tongue. Besides, Dylan was too close to him and could cause him harm.

"I'm not the mushy type, but, well, I love you, you old poop." Again, he had a feeling he'd missed something, but felt like he could let it go for now. "We were just talking about how we need to get a family picture of all of us, and then you invited Tanner to be a part of it. I think that's wonderful. And then you made him and the rest of us very aware of your ideas on his sexuality. You are, as I said, a good man."

"Oh. Well, he'd better be there. And like I told him, it doesn't matter to me what he loves. So long as he's here with us." Tanner nodded. "Also, Flora. Some of you haven't met her yet, but she's the cutest little thing. She's family too."

Dinner was the usual fare. Loud, fun, and full of love. And plenty of food to go around at least twice. Ollie decided that he'd do what his mate wanted him to and stick around until the babies stopped coming. He had a feeling that wouldn't be for a very long time with this group. And he was looking forward to every bit of it.

Chapter 11

Madeline hated waiting, as well as being in the dark about things. This meeting, for instance. She was here to figure out what her brother had left her. She hoped it was enough to pay her fines, whatever they might be, as well as enough left over to have some fun. She looked down at the paper in front of her. It was a lot of shit that she didn't agree with, but had no power to change any of it. Fucking attorneys took everything that she had, and for no good reason.

The house was gone. Not only that, but the contents too. And the money that the sale of it had brought was nothing compared to what she'd put into the place. Why, the bedspread alone in her room was worth a hundred times more than the person who had bought it paid for it. Five bucks. It was sinful.

There were other things on the list as well. Jewelry that she'd gotten at other estate sales. And where she couldn't come to a good price on them, she'd taken them. Also, her shoes. All of those were now on the feet of some bidder with the number fourteen. Madeline hoped that person fell and broke her fool neck for how little she paid for them. One dollar a pair was like stealing them.

"Did you have any questions?" She looked at the man in front of her and tried to remember who he was. "I'm the auctioneer, Andy. I sold the things in the household and then the house. Did you have any questions about the way it went? Also, I don't know if they told you this or not, but someone took pictures of the event. It was well attended, and I think things went for a good price."

"Shows what you know. And yes, I have a few questions. Why did you have the right to sell my things anyway?" He told her that the bank had contacted him and he had agreed to do it to pay her outstanding bills. "So just how do you think my bills are going to be paid by you selling my things for so little? What you should have done was burn it all, and I could have claimed the insurance on it. Your way, this woman here, number fourteen, has all my shoes, and she's going to wear them like she bought them for herself. If you want my opinion, that's just nasty. And I don't like it. Are you going to make up the difference? To the *unpaid* bills for how little you sold my things for? And not for a moment do I believe there are any unpaid anything."

"Number fourteen was a man, at least for now, and he bought them to wear in his new life. I believe that he's a transgender person that is wearing them as part of his new look that he's having done." She asked him what the hell that was. "Transgender? It's a word that denotes or relates to a person whose sense of personal identity and gender does not link with their birth sex. Like they were born a male, like this person, but feels like a woman on the inside. Quite brave of him, if you ask me."

"You mean one of those men who dress up as a woman?" He nodded and smiled. "Are you telling me that you sold my shoes to a man dressing up as a woman? And you did so without my permission? How dare you?"

"I think he bought a few of your dresses as well. He told me he was excited to wear them. I think he's hoping for a fresh start and looking nice too. Or as nice as he can in your clothing." Madeline told him to get them back. "I'm afraid I can't do that. Not that I would even if I could. This person bought them in good faith, and I sold them in the same manner."

"I didn't want them sold in the first place." She knew she was getting louder and tried to calm herself. If she got into trouble again, she'd have to sit in her cell without anyone to talk to. "Those were my things that I bought with my money. How much did this thing net me? I'm thinking not as much as I would have gotten had I been in charge. I need that money to get out of here."

"Get out of here? Lady, you're not leaving here." He stood up. "I'm sorry that you're so disappointed in the sale of your things. Perhaps you should have thought of the consequences before you landed yourself in jail. And the money that was made went to your outstanding bills. And trust me lady, you didn't have enough stuff in that house of yours to even make a dent in all you owe."

He left her sitting here. Damn it, people were going to have to understand that she wasn't the bad guy here. Everyone took money from the places they worked. It might not have been as much as she did, which she thought was overestimated, but everyone did it. A pencil or pen here and there. A sick day with pay without really being ill. Charging a dinner on a credit card that wasn't really business. Everyone did it. Why the hell was she being made an example of? It was completely unfair. Christ, she hated that she'd been caught.

The amount of money that was brought from the sale wasn't all that much, but it would have gone a long way in replacing her things. But the country club took the bulk of it, and the rest went for legal fees they incurred in suing her. Which, to her way of thinking, they could have not sued her and not have the fees in the first place. See? No one thought things over like she did. It was a travesty, that's what it was. She knew for a fact that they had funds for that. Why were they taking them from her?

Then they read her brother's will. Mary was there with another man. She thought at first she was already seeing someone, but it turned out to be her lawyer. Samuel's children hadn't been allowed to come, nor had hers. She missed them, but not enough to put up a fuss about not seeing them. Most of the time they were annoying and loud. The peace and quiet of the cell had been the only good thing about being there. Mary wouldn't even look at her, her face puffy from crying all the time. If she had loved Samuel half as much as Madeline had, Mary would have killed herself too, and saved Madeline the trouble of getting her half of the estate.

It took them ten minutes to get to her part. He'd left her the bulk of his estate, which was good. Now things were going her way. Mary got the insurance policy, the house, and anything in it. Which, she supposed, was nice. Mary wasn't looking any younger, and perhaps she could get herself some tightening here and there to spruce her up with the money from his policy.

But before she could ask anyone information about her

share, she was being carted back to the van. Stopping in the hall, she demanded to know when she was going to get her part of the estate. She wanted to get on with her life.

"Your part goes back to those that the two of you stole from. Mary will get the insurance, but the house will need to be sold to help pay the bills, as well as anything else inside. Your part of it will also go toward the theft that you incurred here and outside of the jail." She shook her head. "You don't get to profit while in jail, Maddie. And the money you stole has to be returned. You were told that. Every time you brought up money, someone told you that it was to pay your part in all this."

"Not by my brother's money. And it's Madeline, not Maddie. I've told you this before." They took her down the hall when the attorney she had stopped and walked away. "It's my money, damn it. He left that all to me."

He'd more than likely stolen it too. But it was hers. She needed to get her own attorney and have him look into things. Or better yet, she needed to get an advance on the money that Alfred was paying them. Of course, he might not have it either, being in jail and all. But Samuel did try to kill Sunshine...that should count for something. Damn it. Nothing seemed to be going her way. And she was getting more and more pissed every time someone told her that she was getting money and she didn't.

"You know, for as much money as people are making off me, someone could at least spring for a limo when I have to have my ass carted around the city for shit. And at the very least, I shouldn't have to be chained up like a dog." No one, of course, said anything. And the cop in the back of the stupid thing only shook his head at her. "You'd think that I was this big king boss or something the way I get treated."

"I never heard one of them complain as much as you do, that's for sure." She wanted to get up and smack the man. "Why don't you do us all a favor and shut—?"

The sound of squealing tires had her looking out the window in the back. The semi was coming at them fast, and all she could think about in that moment was how big the fucker was. Then it hit them.

The van shuddered, then flipped. Her head hit the top then the seat several times as they rolled over and over. It all happened so fast that Madeline hadn't been able to brace herself for impact. Her head hit several more times before it came to a stop. Madeline could only think of how much pain she was in as darkness engulfed her.

When she woke, it was disorientating for her. It appeared that she was still buckled in the back of the van, but as it was now upside down, she was hanging from the top rather than the bottom. She let the buckle go when she realized that she was no longer pinned to the floor, and dropped. Her head hit the ceiling to the van and she was out again.

The next time she woke up, she was lying on the ground. Someone had pulled her out of the wreckage, and she could see several men working on the front of it. Sitting up caused her some pain, but she was free. Standing up, careful of not making any kind of noise, Madeline seized the opportunity to get away. Stupid people wouldn't even miss her, she thought. Laughing to herself, she ran to the first large tree she could see.

Unsure of where she was, Madeline kept close to the road. Several cars drove past her, as well as cruisers and a couple ambulances with lights and sounds going off. She wondered for a moment if the rest of the people had died, but didn't really care. They'd been jerks to her, and she wasn't going to waste her time thinking about them. She was more important right now.

It was getting dark by the time she realized she couldn't see much ahead of her. Madeline didn't want to run into any creatures that might be out lurking for food, so she looked for shelter. She was thinking of the guns that had been on the officers, but knew that her chances of getting them were about as slim as her raising the dead. It would have been nice, she thought, to have been able to protect herself, but she was free so that was better anyway.

"Not sure where that thought came from, but I like it." Giggling, she wondered if she'd hit her head a little too hard, but closed her mouth. Talking, especially out here in the dark, could get her caught.

Madeline came upon the barn as the sun was rising. She had no idea where she was or how far from the accident she'd traveled, but since she'd not seen anyone or heard cars racing along the road, she felt safe. For all she knew she could have been going in circles all night and passed this particular barn several times. Moving into it, terrified of finding a cow or something else that would hurt her, she climbed the stairs to the loft and looked around.

Finding an old blanket in the corner, she was too exhausted to care what shape it was in. She shook it hard and placed it over the sweet-smelling straw. Almost as soon as she laid her head down, her body began to make every little pain known to her. Crying softly, not wanting to disturb anything that might be sharing the straw with her, Madeline decided she would get out of this and get everything she'd had back.

It was time people took notice of her.

When Madeline woke, she had to throw up, and did so without thought to who might be close enough to hear her. Violently she puked up her belly, until she thought for sure she was going to die despite having escaped her imprisonment. When she laid back down she didn't fall asleep again. She knew that she had to get moving soon…she hadn't been all that careful about not leaving a trail for anyone to follow. So, getting up, her belly still rebelling, she made her way down the ladder and into the big barn.

She could see now that it had been empty for some time. Cobwebs hanging in long, branch-like arms would have kept her out had she seen them. But she knew that there had been little to no hope of finding better digs, nor a hotel. Not dressed the way she was.

"It used to be that my name alone would get me into any place I wanted to go. Now I'm reduced to hiding in barns and wearing last year's clothing." At least there was that. She did still have her dress on from the visit today; or yesterday, she supposed now. "Sunshine. I need to go and see her. She'll have to fix me up with money and a way out of town." She had seen the article in the paper about her, and it had mentioned where she was living. It would be a simple thing to find the address of the house.

Blood could easily be explained, if asked. She'd had a bloody nose. Or she'd cut her arm. There wasn't any mirror in the barn, which was something she would have thought there would be. Did the farmer not care that his head might have webs in it? Or if he had hat hair? More and more Madeline wondered how people coped without her around to guide them.

There was still the matter of her not knowing where she was, but that didn't bother her overly much. She had a plan, and while she didn't want to see Sunshine—as she had messed things up for her—she did need her once more. And she would pay or else. Madeline wasn't going to take no for an answer this time. It was high time that Sunshine started taking her big sister seriously. And she would too, even, if she had to kill her to do so.

~~~

All Sunny could think about was that her sister was out there. She didn't think that Madeline would leave her alone, either. She'd come for her and make her pay, however that worked in her head, no matter what. And the fact that she was a wanted woman wouldn't stop her once she got something in her head.

"I just heard from the police. They said that she's been hurt, but they don't know how badly. I'm thinking not too bad, or she wouldn't have been able to get up and go." David pulled her into his arms. "They'll figure this out. I promise. The men that pulled her from the wreckage said they hadn't thought of her being anything but a passenger when they freed her. She wasn't chained up by then, and she was dressed in regular clothing. I'm so sorry."

"Can we go look for her too?" He said that was a bad idea. "So is her being out there. She's going to come here, if for no other reason than to tell me that I have to help her. I won't, but that won't stop her from coming here. I've come to the conclusion that she's nuts, David. Right off her fucking rocker."

"The police are putting in extra patrols, and the pack as well as the leap are watching the family. Going out there after her would be good on one hand, but would bring up so many problems too. Like the fact that we'd kill her without any qualms. Which would raise more questions. I've even sent some of them to look after your in-laws." She thanked him. "No problem, honey. I don't want her hurting anyone."

"Did they say how the accident occurred? She didn't do it, did she? Or pay anyone to have the van wrecked?" He said that he had heard and it wasn't her, but that they'd been rear-ended by a trucker who hadn't seen them until it was too late. "I'm so glad that it wasn't her that caused this. I think that would have been much harder to take. That man and woman that were with her are both dead, and she's out there like nothing happened."

"They were driving down the road when a deer leapt in front of them, causing them to have to stop. That was when they were hit, and it caused them to roll several times before they landed on their top. Both the officers were killed almost instantly, they think." She knew there was a large deer population around there, so that didn't really surprise her. "The men who had stopped to help said that there were at least three dead or dying, and that your sister was unconscious without any apparent broken bones. The driver of the truck wasn't dead then, but he did die later at the hospital."

"Those poor people. All of them lost their lives because of an animal. And it made it so she could escape." He nodded. "Now what? I mean, she escaped. Are they looking for her at all?"

"Yes. And since she escaped from custody, they're adding that to her charges as well." But that only helped keep her away if they found her. And Maddie was forever landing on her feet. She was as bad as a...well, she was going to say cat, but she was nothing like that. "What are you thinking?"

"That I'd like to shift and take a run. I think that I need it." She'd been changed two days ago and needed to feel the cat. She was there, but Sunny had never been her yet. "What do you think?"

"Evan said we should wait for a bit. He didn't say how long, but he's worried because you lost so much blood." She had too. The bed that she'd been on had been so badly covered in her blood that they'd had to purchase a new one. "But if you feel like it, we can go. So long as you're careful and rest a lot. We need you healthy for the baby."

A baby. She was going to have a baby, and was so happy and excited that she would wake up in the middle of the night and hold herself. She could not wait to touch her little boy or girl. And having it with the one person in the world she loved more than herself was the best part of this.

"I know you have been told this, but I want you to remember, no running too much. Not yet at any rate. I'm not being overprotective, but I don't want anything to wear you out either. Also, you're going to be overwhelmed by the scents you'll smell. Remember this morning when you could smell the cut flowers that were brought in? Well, this will be stronger." She nodded. It had been the strangest thing to be able to smell everything at once. "Also, there are wolves as well as tigers roaming around. The tigers are easy to tell who they are—there aren't any wild ones around—but the wolves look like their wild counterparts, only bigger. All right?"

"Yes. Tell me what to do." He told her. "So, I think of her, that's all? Just think of her and she'll come to me?"

"Yes. Just be careful." She closed her eyes, thinking this was the strangest thing she'd ever done, and she saw her.

"See her?"

"Yes. She's beautiful." Sunny wondered if she should tell him that she was all white, but decided that might not be right. "I'm going to call to her."

The shift wasn't painful at all. It was quick too, much faster than she had it in her head it would be. And even though she'd seen David do it a lot, it was still something that she thought would be harder and longer the first time. Opening her eyes, she looked at David and watched his face. She didn't think there was such a thing as an ugly tiger, but she had no idea. He sat down on the chair and smiled.

"You're a ghost tiger. I think that's what Mom used to call them. All white but for the stripes. I've heard them called snow tigers as well. It means luck to the family. I don't know if I could be any luckier, having you as my mate, but my grandda is going to have a brick. Maybe two of them." She asked him if she was all right. "All right? You're beautiful. And mine."

I've always been yours, I think. I just had to find you first. He nodded and rubbed his hand over her head. *I want to run. I need to for some reason. It's like my body is humming with it. Is that okay? That I go?*

"Go. I'll be there in a minute. I want to take some pictures too." She nodded and posed for him a few times. "All right, love. You run and I'll chase you down. Be careful."

She promised that she would and took off. It took her a few steps to remember that she wasn't on two feet, but once she got the hang of it, she made her way to the tree line. Beyond there, she knew a whole world was going to open for her. And Sunny was as excited about that as she was an assignment that she was first starting out with.

144

There were a great many scents for her to smell. Branches of bushes were covered in the scent that she thought was deer. A wolf had come through her way too. Smelling a flower that was struggling to push up from the fallen leaves, she could smell someone had peed on it and it made her sneeze.

One of the wolves is letting us know that he's been here. She pointed out that he'd peed on a little flower. *Probably not the flower, but he might have dribbled on it. He was more than likely aiming for the bush. He's just like all males, and his aim isn't as good as he might think.*

She thought that was gross too. Moving on, she realized he could see her and turned. There her big tiger stood, his body sitting against a tree while he watched her. She told him he was beautiful too.

I've never seen you up and walking. Every time you shift, it's in our room and you're in bed with me. I knew you'd be big, I just never realized how big you'd be. He stayed where he was. *Why aren't you running with me? Or at least coming along? Is something out here?*

My tiger is worried about you. He knows that you're breeding, and he's keeping an eye on you two. She told him how romantic that was. *Yes, well, he's also afraid of you. He knows that he hurt you, and he doesn't want you to be upset with him. While it seems as if we're one person that just happens to be able to turn into an animal, he has his thoughts just as I do.*

Tell him that I'm not mad at him. In fact, I love being a tiger. I don't know what happened, but I love it. She felt the air around her tense up and she looked around. David, as his tiger, came to her and stood so close that she could feel his heat. *Something is here. I don't know what it was, but something magical just happened.*

"It is I, Tanner." The little fae on his shoulder came to stand between her and David. "She wishes to get your scent as your felines. Also, I have heard about your changing. I'm so sorry about that. I might have...my blood might have had something to do with what happened. I've also come to tell you that your sister is nearby. I don't know where, I've never had her scent, but she has been spotted by some of my friends. I've come to give you a heads up. Also, to let you know that there are more than just the ones that you can see here among your woods. There are eyes watching over you all the time."

She wasn't sure that she could talk to him so she started to shift, then remembered that she would be naked. Waiting to see what she should do now, Sunny realized that David was talking to Tanner when he spoke again.

"You have my blood, young Sunny. You may speak to me at any time, even in my slumber. It works the same as it would with David and the other cats you know." She asked him about the fae. "Flora. She's been with me for as long as I've been a vampire. We need one another, more, sometimes, than either of us admit."

The fae, Flora spoke to them then. Her voice was musical. And she had an accent, a heavy French one. It was beautiful the way she spoke to them. "There are many more of my kind. We're very protective of those that we love, and I know of two that wish to be with you at all times. Especially with the young tigers coming along. Would you consent to that?" Sunny looked at David, who nodded. "Thank you. I will send them along soon. They will protect you like nothing else can, my lady. And then the babies that come along as well."

Thank you, Flora. I'm glad for the protection. She bowed before going back to stand on Tanner's shoulder. *Thank you both for being here for us. And for telling us about my sister. I'm afraid for my new family.*

"As you should be." Tanner bowed too. "We shall leave you to your run. Enjoy. Oh, and David, her body is in good shape. You need have no other worries about her changing. She is going to be just fine."

When they both were gone, David showed her how to smell for things, like fresh water and plants she could eat if necessary. The entire time, he never left her side or treated her with anything but respect. It was like having her best friend and lover all at the same time. She really did love this man, and was so happy that they had found each other.

The woods were like a new book for her. So many stories she could tell from each plant that she touched. The water where other animals stopped to take a drink. She heard sounds from other creatures that she'd never encountered before, and she was able to see things she'd never noticed with her human eyes. It was wonderful, this whole new place she was getting to know, and she hated to go inside. She felt like a small child who was being denied just one more swing on the playground, or a little further out on the bike.

How about I make it up to you? She asked David what he had in mind. Then he shifted to his other half when she did and finished his answer. "How about I take you upstairs, give you a nice bath, then make love to you for the rest of the night?"

"Sounds like a plan." They were headed to their room when she remembered a phone call she'd gotten earlier. "I have another job. I'm going to look into some spillage in the county waste department. Apparently, it's messing with the lakes and fish."

"You'll go with someone? I mean, someone that can watch out for you while you're doing your job? I know that you can take care of yourself, but with Maddie around, I don't want you to take any chances. After she's taken care of, then you can only take one other person with you." She said she didn't know anyone that would like to sit around while she worked. It was sort of boring for the most part. "Okay, would it be all right if I sent someone along? Just in case? Maybe one of my brothers, perhaps?"

"Sure. I don't mind. But if they get in my way, your head will roll." They were laughing when they entered the bedroom and she stopped in the door. "Oh, David. How wonderful."

The room was covered in roses of every color imaginable. Vases of them on the dressers. There were some lying on the bed, petals as well. She took the one he handed her and smelled it. It smelled absolutely wonderful. There was a bucket of champagne near the bed, the condensation dripping to the floor and onto more roses. A huge box of chocolate that had a large red bow on the lid was opened, the sweet confections begging to be sampled. He kissed her on the cheek and then handed her a small blue box while on bended knee.

"Sunshine, will you become my wife for all eternity? Love me no matter how stupid I act, and keep me happy forever?" She nodded. "I love you so very much. And my heart only beats for you, and will be yours long after death, if we ever die."

"I love you." And she proceeded to show him just how much.

Chapter 12

The book was coming along. David thought he might have it done well before the deadline, and was thinking of the pictures he wanted to incorporate in the novel as he finished up the chapter he was on. While not his usual genre, he was having a great time with it, and thought he'd like to do this more often. Not all the time, but just on occasion when a place took his fancy.

There were hundreds of pictures now. With the information that Sunny had given him from touching some of the items, he'd found names that he'd not had before, as well as birth certificates and wedding licenses on file. He loved that everything he was finding about the old house was as accurate as anything he'd ever done before. Of course, there was little truth in some of the other books he wrote, but for this, he wanted accuracy.

David's usual genre was romance. Not the kind that someone would find in the library, but things that were more suited to brown paper bags and nightlight reading.

His mom told him after reading his first one that she wasn't going to read anymore. It was too much to think of her little boy writing such things. They were good, she told him, but not from her son. He laughed all the way home. It was the greatest compliment he thought he'd ever received. He didn't even mind that she wasn't going to read others. Just knowing that she had one made him feel great.

Starting on the next chapter, he looked at the notes he'd written down. Rarely did he use any, nor an outline when writing, but with this, he had to. Not only to keep all the names straight and who had married who, but also timelines. There was only one, just the couple that owned the house during the time that he was writing about, but so much had occurred during that time, he wanted to make sure that he got it right. And weaving the others, the slaves and house help that they saved, in and out of their lives was an extra element of complication. The kind that he loved.

David was in a zone when the doorbell rang. He wasn't sure that anyone else was home…Sunny had gone out at dawn to see about the spillage, and they'd only just hired a cook to help out. He'd sent Adam with her, as he knew the land better than she did, and he would watch over her. David felt comfortable with the two of them going out, and had been busy working since she'd gone. Now this.

When the doorbell rang again, he went to the door. He hadn't been in the habit of looking before opening the door, and didn't do it this time. As soon as he saw her, he knew that he'd be checking from now on before swinging a door wide to whoever wanted to come in.

"Maddie. What are you doing here? I was hoping that you would be back in prison by now." The gun was pointed right at his heart or he might have tried to knock it away from her. Then there was the added frightening fact that she was as steady as a rock holding it. "You're not helping yourself by doing this. I'm sure that you're aware of that, aren't you?"

"Yes, well, my plans for that have changed. Where is Sunshine? She needs to give me some money and a car. And don't tell me that she doesn't have it. Living in this big house, there has to be someone with cash supplying it. Do you sell drugs or something, David? I don't believe that you're really her husband, but since you're going to give me money, I'll believe whatever you want." He told her that she wasn't there. "Well, then you give it to me. I'm, as you can guess, in sort of a hurry, so if you could get to it, I won't have to shoot you. I might anyway. There isn't any reason whatsoever that Sunshine should have more than me. Don't you agree?"

"I'm not going to give you money. Nor a car, even if I had one to give you." The shot to his arm nearly had him falling to the floor. But the pain was nothing compared to the need to kill her. "What the fuck did you do that for?"

"Well, in the event you don't know this, I'm not really a nice person. And I don't like you. You think you're all high and mighty, and I want to destroy you. Right along with my sister. Who, you might have guessed, is a bitch of the highest order. I don't like her either." The second shot had him reaching out to his family. Any and all of them. "What do you think my dear sister will do when she comes home to find you dead? I'm hoping that it makes her very cooperative. However, I'm betting that she comes after me. But with my trusty weapon here, I can end that quickly enough. Give me the money and car and I'll just let you bleed out."

He was going down fast when the third bullet ripped

through his belly. Shifting after the second shot, the one that hit him in the chest, might have killed him. It would for sure now. He felt his family speaking to him, but there wasn't any way for him to talk back. David was lying in a pool of his own blood when he heard a scream.

Someone touched him, his face, and he tried to open his eyes. But he was having a hard enough time breathing around the pain, much less focusing on a person. He could see her, her tiny face and hands, but nothing else. It was the fae, that was all he could remember before darkness took him.

~~~

Tanner didn't move from his place near the bed. He was actually afraid to draw attention to himself. The men in the room, all of them on the verge of shifting in their anger, would not mean to harm him, but they would, simply because he was there.

The sun was bright in the room now…it hadn't been when he sat here. But he'd no more leave this room now than he would these men. They needed him, if only for someone to keep them safe and away from the gory mess below.

He'd only seen the aftermath of the encounter, and that was enough to convince him that he didn't want to know details. Knowing that the woman was dead was enough for him. For now. He looked at Flora when she moved to sit upon the man in the bed.

"He will live." Tanner told her that he knew that. "And the mate, she'll be all right now as well. Do you think that she will be upset with me?"

"Whatever for?" She shrugged. "Do you feel as if you did something wrong here today? You saved her mate from being badly hurt, and I think that will be all that she will think about.

You did what no one else could have, Flora…you saved her mate from certain death. She will praise your name daily, I think."

"I killed her sister." Tanner knew that. "Not nicely either. She suffered. Greatly. I made sure of it. I will tell her should she ask or you tell me to, but I think it best that she does not ever know. It will hurt her, I think, knowing that she suffered at my hands."

"You did what you felt you needed to." He wasn't sure before that he wanted to know, but in the event that he was asked, he thought it might be better if he did. "What did you do to her, Flora?"

He could have gone to get Sunny and bring her home with his magic. But it was daylight out, and he wasn't sure if he'd cause her more harm than good by his bringing her that way. He wasn't weak, not really, but he'd not been feeding well, and knew that he wasn't at his best. Tanner was depressed, and this situation with the woman that had come here today was bad. He didn't want anyone to suffer, but this was an evil necessity.

"She had already shot him by the time I got to him. She… she meant for him to be dead when Sunny returned. I could not allow that." No, he told her, she could not have allowed that. "I entered her body, in the same way that she did his with the bullets, leaving bits of me behind."

He took a moment to understand why she'd do such a thing. "You wanted her to live longer while you did what you needed to." She nodded. "Go on, Flora. Tell me what you did to the human."

"She had to suffer. I entered her body over and over, leaving less and less of me inside of her. And when she was nothing more than a mass of human flesh, I removed her head and then left her there to attend to Master David." He asked her how long this had taken her. "Seconds. Mere seconds to end her life. But to her, I would imagine that it seemed much longer, do you not think so? She did not deserve to breathe the same air as them. I needed to make her gone, Tanner. You know that, do you not?"

Nodding, he looked around the room. The men were quiet; they'd not heard them speaking, nor would they have seen the little fae. Tanner wondered what they had thought, coming into the big house and finding their brother lying on the floor bleeding, and the body of his sister-in-law barely recognizable as a human. He shuddered when he thought of the amount of energy and magic that it would have taken the little fae to have done such a thing. And in only seconds, as she had said.

"Tanner?" He looked at Evan when he said his name. "Do you know what happened to her? And to my brother?"

"Yes." Evan, as good as man as he'd ever known, sat down beside him. "I think it is best that you do not know what happened. She is dead, and the police will be here soon. They will see nothing but a body. And thanks to the magic of my fae, he will live for a great long time. This is…he is resting now, as that is what he needs, but he will be fine."

"The fae, your friend, she did it." Nodding, he didn't look at Flora, not wanting him to know she was there in the event that he was upset. "The next time you see her, will you tell her that I am eternally grateful for what she did for us? Had she not been here.... Well, I'm so happy that she did what she did. And you too, for what the police are going to see."

They arrived then. To him it looked as if the entire police

department was on the lawn. The manhunt for the woman had ended, and each of them wanted to be a part of her capture, even though they all knew that she was dead. He didn't leave the room, electing to stay with young David in case he woke. Evan and the others left him and David's mother there to deal with the aftermath.

"I've spoken to Sunny. She's in a tizzy, as you can well imagine." Tanner asked if she was aware that David was all right. "Yes, but until she sees him, much like me, she won't believe it. I think she's thinking that we're going to be upset with her."

"Why?" He understood as soon as the word left his mouth. "Because it was her sister that harmed him. I can understand her thinking that, can you not? But she has nothing to worry about. We all love the woman dearly."

"Yes. But I hurt for her. Both her siblings are gone now. And only in a matter of a few days. I'd be devastated, but her family wasn't at all like most. To be honest with you, Tanner, I'm glad that they're gone. They were terrible people, and they would have continued to hurt her, even if this other stuff hadn't come along. To think that they shared the same blood." Tanner agreed with her. "She'll need us all now, I think. More so than before. I worry for the child she carries too."

Tanner only thought for a second before he looked at Flora. There was much he could tell the elder Whitfield, a great many things that she could look forward to as well as find tragic. But hope, he knew, could go a long way to healing even the most horrific of hurts.

"The children of Evan and Dylan will arrive soon." She said that they were only watching out for them for the county. "Yes, but it will be more. They'll adopt them, but in order for that to happen, you must take a stand against them. The children will need you to be the hand that heals and hurts."

"You don't mean that I'll have to harm those children, do you?" He nodded. "I can no more do that than I could raise a hand against you, Tanner. What a thing to tell me. I've never even raised a hand to my own children, much less grandchildren."

"Then all will be lost." She stared at him for several seconds before she looked at her son. "He will be fine. Once he wakes, he'll not even be weak. Flora helped him in ways that you cannot imagine, my dear lady."

She didn't comment. He knew that her thoughts were still on the children. They were good boys, the two coming to the leap leader, but they also had been through a great deal, and needed someone to put them into a good place. Dylan could do it, and would, but she'd not know how to begin. Eve would be able to not only straighten them out, but would also love them more than anyone else could.

"They're set to come here this afternoon. I've thought about calling the home and asking that it be put off. At least for a couple of days." He said nothing, knowing that if she did that, the younger boy would die. "I won't now. They'll need us, and perhaps we'll need a bit of distraction. They might be the balm that brings us out of this."

"Mom?" David sat up but didn't move off the bed. "She's here. You have to call the others."

"She's gone. Maddie has been taken care of, son." He looked confused, but then nodded. "Are you all right? I know that you were hurt badly, but you seem to be all right. You are, aren't you? Oh, and Sunny is on her way home. We thought it best that she come here when you were awake. She's frantic with worry about you."

"I've spoken to her, just now. She's nearly here, and sorry about what had happened. She's blaming herself for Maddie coming here and doing this. I told her that no one would ever blame her for what her sister did." David looked at Tanner. "She saved my life. Flora, she was there and saved my life. I don't remember much, but her face was there with me; she held me."

"Yes, she did." Tanner stood up then. It was time he took his leave. "I will return later in the day, once the sun has gone down. Should you need me, for any reason, just call. I will come to you."

"Thank you. And tell Flora that I owe her my life." He told David that she didn't see it that way, but would tell her. The little fae nodded when he glanced at her. "I'd like to pay her back in some way, Tanner. Tell her that for me."

"I shall, young David, but again, I don't think she'll see that you owe her anything." He made his way to the door, but paused when he realized that Flora had left the room, more than likely in their rooms below by now. He felt as if he could speak without her hearing him. "If I were you, I'd think of picking a fae for yourself and Sunny from the ones that will come to see you soon. They can be most useful when you are in need. And if you are insistent in repaying Flora, I'm sure that there are any number of flowers you could plant for her."

He came out of the room, closing the door behind him when he saw her on the staircase. She was just sitting there, waiting for him. After telling her that he was ready, she rode on his shoulder as they made their way, magically, down to the lower levels. It had been a long afternoon, and would be a short night for him. When he laid upon his bed, Flora sat beside him.

"They will not give up on repaying you. You should think of something that you'd like to have, something that they can do for you to settle their hearts." She nodded. "It is only early fall, but time enough for them to plant you your own garden. Or something along that line. It would go a long way in them not pestering you for such a gift."

"I would like that." But he could tell she had something else in mind. "Do you remember the gardens that I was working on with Adam? Do you think they'd let me be in charge of them? To see what I can grow and care for? I should not do anything without their permission, but Adam, he said that the gardens were much more than he had first thought, and didn't know if he had the time to devote to it."

"I think that would be something they'd love to allow you to run. They too have little time to devote to the grounds like you would. With the children coming, there will be less time than now." She smiled at him. "You have already made it your own in your heart, haven't you, my dear?"

"Yes, in a way. I have planted some seeds that have long since been thought of as gone. And a few of the roots there, they needed but a little magic to come forth. It will be a grand garden even without me working much on it." He nodded as he began to prepare for his rest. "Tanner, do you think we could find us a home? One that we could live in with this family forever? If you do not wish it, I would understand."

"I think I should like that very much. I have made arrangements to find us one. And it will feel as if we're closer to Fredrick here than if we were at home." She nodded and looked to the small window that she'd put into the wall for herself to come and go. "I shall be fine here, if you should like to leave me. There are many here that would warn me should there be trouble."

"You are a good master, Tanner. I don't know what I would have done had you not rescued me that day." He said for her not to speak of such a terrible thing. "Still, he was set to take my wings off and then smash me. I would have died but for you. I thank you."

"And I thank you, Flora, for being my friend and companion for all these centuries." He closed his eyes as he continued. "I love you, my dear. Very much so."

She left him then, going off to work in the gardens that she so loved. He would speak to Evan about such a gift. It would be no trouble for them to hand it over to her, more than likely something that they'd gladly do. But he also knew that they'd think it not enough, and that was the reason that he loved this family so much.

Reaching out once more before he rested, he told Evan and Dylan what was talked about. Evan, of course, was all for it, and Dylan thought they could do more. And would. She had a suggestion that would make his fae the envy of every other creature around. And her heart would be so full that he knew she'd feel as if they'd given her too much. She would love it, but it would be too much in her mind.

I'll take care of it today for her. It'll be our pleasure. Tanner said thank you, and Dylan laughed. *If only things were always this easy. My life would be decidedly boring.*

He doubted that would ever be a problem for this young woman. Dylan was in the middle of a great many things, and would continue to be. She was someone that got things done, and did them well. He let sleep take him as soon as he closed the connection. He was going to need rest to deal with this family.

~~~

There was little to do about it now but wait. The boys were to arrive in a little while, and Eve still hadn't figured out what she was going to do. Not that she had much information, but she would have to take a stand. And for some reason she had a feeling that would set the tone for the rest of their lives and hers. Another thought had occurred to her, but she wasn't sure what to think of that. Not today at any rate.

One or both of them would die. Eve didn't know why that thought kept coming to her, but she knew it was as true as anything she might have thought of before. One of those young boys would need her to do this or they'd die. Tanner had not told her that, but his tone and the fact that he said all would be lost made her think it. Every second since he'd said it.

Almost as soon as they were in the door, she could see that they were going to be trouble. Not that she thought it was something that would get them killed, but Eve couldn't shake the feeling that she had to do something. And when the older of the two boys, Kyle was his name, got smart with Dylan for the second time, she walked right up to him and slapped him hard across the face.

The print from her hand was there for everyone to see. No one spoke, not even the boy, when she knew it was on the tip of his tongue to tell her off. But before anyone could tell her she was wrong, she snapped her fingers at him and told him to behave.

He was angry, but hurt too, she could see that. But she gave him no quarter and drew back to hit him again should he need it. Dylan, thankfully, stepped back.

"You talk to anyone in your family like that again and I will make sure you're taken to the woodshed. Do you understand me?" He glared and said nothing. "I asked you a question, young man, and I demand an answer."

"You hit me." She said that she did and would again if he didn't straighten up. "You think you're all that? Well, I won't stay here where somebody can just take shots at a kid and think to get away with it. I'm leaving."

Going to the door, she opened it for him. "There you go. Go then. You think we want a smart assed person in this family? We don't. You have a reason for being upset, then we can talk about it. But there is no cause, none whatsoever, that you be a smart mouth to the couple who would give their lives for you. Any of us would. Now, you tell her you're sorry for being that way or I will take you out back myself."

"They don't know me." Eve told him that he'd not given anyone any information other than to be mean. "And if I leave here, what is it you're going to do about it? Turn me in to the cops?"

"Should I?" He shrugged. "Don't give me that sort of answer. Tell me, have you done something wrong that would warrant me having to call the police on you? To be honest with you, I've seen the back end of enough cops today. It's been a terrible day here too. Well? Do I need to call them?"

"No, ma'am. I don't want to be hurt again." She asked him if he meant by her or out in the world. "Both. My dad, he's dead. My momma is gone too. She left us all alone to fend for ourselves, and we did a crappy job of it."

"Did you? From where I'm standing, you're doing a good job, other than the attitude you seemed to have developed. You and your brother are still alive, aren't you? And I would imagine that it was mostly due to your keeping you safe. But you need help, and it's here if you wish it." He nodded and dropped his head. "Look at me when I'm speaking to you."

"I don't know what to do." She moved toward him slowly, like he was a wounded animal that had no idea how to react to kindness. "They hurt us. All the time. We tried to be good, but they didn't want us around. It was like living with eight different people, and you just didn't know which one of them was going to come out swinging. And they all did, too. I don't want to live like that anymore."

"You're very welcome here, Kyle. You and your brother. We've been preparing for you for weeks now. And no one here wants you to be hurt. But we will not tolerate being rude. As I said before, we talk about things, not resort to being mean. All right?" He nodded and she lifted his chin up so that he could see her face. "You're my grandson now, both of you, as far as I'm concerned. And I'll treat you as such if you'll allow it. Like giving you hugs when we both need them. Or just when we're together. Would that be all right?"

"Yes, ma'am. Hugging though, it came with a hurt sometimes." She told him not from her. "All right. But not too hard, okay? I'm still hurting myself. They had us checked out, but there are some bruises that we both still have."

"I heard that you'd been beaten. I'm sorry about that. And I hurt badly from the violence that I laid on your handsome face too. But I wanted you to know that we won't have you treating us badly just because you're having a bad time of it." He hugged her, tightly, as she held him back. "My goodness, that is the best hug I've gotten in a very long time. Thank you."

Elliott hugged her too. It was wonderful to be held by

them, but she pulled back to have a look at them both. They were handsome young men, and she was glad that they were going to be with them as family.

"You owe Dylan and Evan an apology, I think. Now, Dylan here, she is a good person, but has a bit of trouble relating to people on a hugging level. So, with her, I'd ask before giving her one. Evan, he's my oldest son, he loves them, giving or receiving them, as much as I do." Elliott asked how many kids she had. "Eight counting wives. Six of them are my sons, and two of the most amazing women you could ever want to have on your side. And my husband, Oliver, and his father, a wonderful man as well, Ollie. You boys have a nice large family to call your own now. Aunts and uncles. Grandparents, as well as a great grandda. You have a few honorary members too, but we'll get to them. There are a lot of things going on around here that you have to be made aware of."

Evan took them up to show them their rooms, and Dylan stared at her. There was something on her mind so Eve waited. When she laughed, Eve smiled.

"Tanner told you something." Eve only smiled bigger. "And this show of force, it had to come from you for what reason? Not that I mind, I was just wondering."

"I don't know what you're talking about. I saw that he was mistreating you and I stepped in." Dylan nodded. "I know you can take care of it, but I just didn't want him to be terrified that you'd draw your gun on him so soon after coming here. You are a wonderful person, Dylan, but your habit of killing first then not having anyone to question later is a bit taxing on friendships. You are going to keep them, aren't you?"

"I don't know how you knew, but we got news this afternoon that they're adoptable. Their mother was found, and she is going to prison for murdering her old man, as she called him. So yes, we're going to take them in. Thank you, Eve." Eve nodded. "I'd like to talk to you about this supposed woodshed. I don't believe for a moment that you have ever once had to take these boys to task. They're terrified of you, and you know it."

"As it should be. And there was nothing to it. Just showing Kyle that we mean business."

She made her way home after that. David was on the mend and her family was growing. Not much more to do than to go home and bake a pie. Eve decided to bake several, just in case someone wanted to come over for dinner tonight.

Chapter 13

Sunny hadn't left his side since she'd gotten home. He loved having her so near, but she wasn't happy. Anyone could see it, and he as well as his family was worried about her. As he sat holding her hand and looking over their backyard, he wondered what he would have to do to shake her out of this funk she was in.

"Dylan said that the boys are settling in very well. I guess Mom had to step in and take one of them to task, but they're good boys." She nodded. "I thought perhaps you and I could adopt one or two in the future."

"I might not be what they need." He asked her what she meant, but she didn't answer him. "Are you sure you want to have this baby? I mean, you never know what sort of person they might turn out to be. There is a lot of crazy shit that has gone on with my family, and maybe they'll be that way too. You don't want that."

He knew; in that moment, he knew what she was thinking. In her mind, she came from bad seeds and didn't want to pass that on to their children. Instead of telling her that she would be a great mom and that they had nothing to worry about, he decided to play the cards his mom did.

"We could put it up for adoption as soon as it's born. That way we won't have to deal with it if it turns out to be a monster." She nodded and looked away. "Of course, we won't know. I mean, for all we know it could be worse than your family was. Or, heaven forbid, like mine."

"What's wrong with your family?" He didn't have an answer, so he didn't give her one. "Your parents have done a great job raising you guys to be good men. And Ollie? Well, I think I love him more than I ever did my own grandparents. Your brothers are amazing too. You're just nuts if you think that they're not good people."

"Sure, but they're not your mate." She nodded. "Do you want to get rid of our child, Sunny? Give it up?"

"What if it really is like my side of the family? They were killers and thieves. They stole so much and did so much harm to their own children and me. Not to mention what they did to all those people that they took things from. And Maddie didn't seem to have a problem in the world with what she'd done, but came here to demand that I pay it off for her. David, I don't want our child to be like that." He told her it was much too late for that now. "No, it's not. I know someone that could take care of it."

"Is that what you want?" She shook her head. "Neither do I. I want us to have this child and love it. Us loving it will be what makes it a special person, don't you think? And even if it tries to become someone like your family, which I highly doubt it will, then we'll take it out to the woodshed that my mom was threatening Kyle with. How about that?"

"She tried to kill you." He said that she had tried but that she hadn't succeeded. "What if Flora hadn't been here? What if she had shot you again? You would have died, we both know it. Even immortal, you wouldn't have been able to survive without blood in your body."

"You can 'what if' things to death, Sunny, but she was here and your sister didn't kill me. I'm alive and healthy. She's gone, never to be heard of again, and we can get on with our lives. And I want to. With you and our child." She nodded again. "Sunny, we're going to have a good time. We'll be fine. I promise you."

"I'm afraid." He said that he was as well, but not about their child. "What if it's like Sam or Maddie? What will we do?"

"What if it's just like you? Or me? Or any member of my family? And if it's not, then we'll love it and guide it in the right direction. We'll all do that...every one of us will be there for each child." She nodded, but didn't look convinced. David decided to change the subject. "I finished my book, thanks to you. I only have to go over some of the edits that I found and add the pictures. I'm having someone come out tomorrow to take a picture of the house as it looks now to use as the cover, and a before and after picture. It's spectacular now. Are you ready to do the hunt with Evan and Dylan?"

"Oh yes." The plan was for them to go along the same route as the map said, and Sunny would show them where the treasures were. "Do you think there will be anything after all this time? I mean, who knows what it'll be, but after all this time, do you think there is anything left worth salvaging?"

"I don't know, but it'll be fun. And a good thing for the boys to get in on. They're excited to be living in a house like that. And no matter what we find, it'll be something that we might not have ever found without you." She nodded and he told her he loved her. "So very much that I ache with it."

"And I love you too. When are we supposed to meet them?" He told her at six. "Then we have time to go for a run, and there will be no biting. All right?"

He stood up and took his shirt off. The air was a little chilly, but his cat wouldn't mind. As soon as he was down to his bare skin, he looked at Sunny. Christ, she was gloriously naked and her body was bright with need.

"I love you." She moved toward him, her steps measured and sure. "If you touch me now, we'll never make it to the woods. I'm seriously needy."

When she dropped to her knees in front of him, he moaned. She'd not even touched him yet and his cock was hurting to come in her mouth. The moment that she touched him, cupped his balls in her warm hand, he knew he was a goner. And when he entered her hot mouth, he cried out with the pure pleasure of it.

David fucked her gently, then hard. The more he got of her, the more he wanted. She was a goddess to him, the only thing in this world that mattered. And when she slid her hand down her belly, all he could think about was that their child was there. His child was growing in her body.

Watching her fingers play with her pussy, he felt his body stiffen with the need to fill her. She moaned longer; her hot breath on his cock when she pulled free made him hurt. He wanted to watch her play, his cum to spray all over her. He held her head in his hand as he took his own pleasure as she gave herself her own.

Come for me. He tried to hold off, but either her command

was too much or she was, but he came hard, filling her mouth and throat with all that he could. When she pulled back from him, he held his cock in his hand and fisted himself until he came all over her body, mouth, and face. It hurt him, like he'd been run through a small hole and come out the other side when he was finished. Then she stood up.

His cat simply took him. And when he lunged for her heat, he didn't slow him down. She needed it, needed them as much as he had her. And when she cried out that she was coming, the cat in him purred and brought her again and again.

Laying back on the deck, his cat moved over her, his mouth devouring her pussy and all her nectar. Sunny came three times, giving him almost more than he could swallow before she begged him to stop. And when he did, taking his body back, he moved up her body slowly and entered her like he had dozens of times before.

"I love you." She moaned at his statement, holding him to her as she came twice more. "You are the best thing that has ever happened to me. And we'll be happy forever."

"Yes, we will." He told her no more talk about their child like that. She would be perfect in every way. "A girl? You want a girl first?"

"Oh yes, just like her mother in every way possible." He took her hard then, his body needing to mark his mate. "Come, Sunny, come with me."

She screamed out his name, her body hard with her release. And when he came too, filling her once again with his cum, she held him so tightly to her body that he could barely breathe. It was then that he felt a deep connection to his mate, and their child. It was indeed a little girl.

They staggered into the house around five-thirty. They didn't have a lot of time left before meeting his brother, so they dressed quickly and warmly. He asked her if she was all right now.

"Yes, better than before. I think I needed to just feel alive." David could understand that and told her so. "I'm still afraid...not sure why, but I am. I think I have a better handle on it; talking to you, having you near me, it helped a great deal. So much has happened in the last few weeks, I just don't know if I can take much more. Do you understand?"

"I do. And I know, on some level, how you feel. When my grandma died, it was devastating to us all. Grandda too, but she was our rock, the foundation that kept us all here and together. When she died, it was like we all lost some of the spark in our lives. Nothing seemed to go right." She told him that was it exactly. "Then you and Dylan came along. And every day, it seems as if the world is a little brighter. It's easier to handle things too...not just normal stuff, but harder ones too because we have each other. Your world was rocked because the people you should have been able to depend on were the ones putting you in that impossible place."

"Yes, that's it. They were never there for me, but this seemed to make it clearer that they weren't. I wanted what you have." He told her she had it now. "I do. I really do."

They arrived at the house a few minutes after six. Kyle and Elliott were ready to go. He asked if they were excited, and Elliott said that they were. Kyle just stared at him. It was then that he realized that Evan would have told them what they were. He asked if he was afraid of him.

"No, I don't think so. But you're all really tigers? Like the big cats in the zoo?" He said they were bigger, but yes, they were. "I believe you, but it's really strange to realize, I think. Evan shifted for us and it was freaky wild. I know the rules, but it was amazing to think he can do that. And we met with Flora too. Tomorrow Tanner is coming over and we'll give him a drop of our blood so he can find us. I don't want to get lost, but it's great knowing that there are so many ways that we can be found. Then the wolf pack is coming by too. So many things that we never knew about, and they're right here in our new family."

"Sunny can shift as well." Kyle looked at her and smiled. "She's not been a cat since birth, so her cat is just a little smaller than a born one. But the pack is all around us now. Protecting us as a payment for us allowing them to be on our grounds. It's a good trade, don't you think?"

"My dad said that it was all hooey about shifters and stuff. I didn't believe him, but he sure did make his point well." David nodded, knowing that the boys had been hurt before. When Kyle moved closer to him, he was surprised by his whispered statement. "I've never been so full before that I had to push food away. And there is always some here."

"You go to my mom's house and you'll think you're going to explode, she has so much. And her pies and cakes? Man, you'll think you've gone on to heaven they're so good." He grinned at him. "Wait until Thanksgiving, Kyle. There is where the real test of your manhood will be. Whether or not you can make it to the couch after the meal to snooze while the game is playing. None of us make it very far after that."

As they made their way on the path they were taking, Kyle and Elliott both asked everyone a lot of questions. Mostly to do with the cats, but they also wanted to know what they should call him. Sunny answered before he could.

"I'm Sunny and he's David. I don't care if you call me aunt or not, that's up to you and your parents." Kyle looked at Evan and Dylan before turning back to them. "However, if you don't call when you need us, I'm going to kick your asses. Understand?"

"Yes, ma'am. Grandma said the same thing. I don't know if you're kidding or not, but I don't think Grandma was. And Great Grandda is funny. He said come spring, he'd take us fishing. I've never even held a pole before." David wondered how his mom was taking that, being called Grandma, and was sure she was loving it. "We both have promised to keep the family secret and to have fun again. I have never been told that before."

"Well, it's good advice, I think." They moved along until Sunny stopped them. "This is the first one. I can feel it here. The map says that it's in the tree beside the fence line."

The stone fence had been found when the yard was being cleaned up. There was another in the back, near the roses, that had also been discovered. Each of them took an area, and Sunny read the instructions once again.

They had a metal detector, as well as a couple of shovels. But on this first treasure, as they were calling it, they had only to climb the tree. Perhaps the items had been lower some time ago, but as the tree grew, they'd been raised up as well. It took them ten minutes to find the first of many, he hoped.

Money. There wasn't a great deal of it, and it was old and frayed. It had been wrapped up in a leather sack that was in much better shape than the paper money. The coins had varying dates, but all were before nineteen hundred. Kyle marked the bag as to where they found it, and Elliott cataloged it in his book. They were on an adventure, it seemed.

They ended up with tattered clothing, coins that were very old, some maps that helped get to the next point, and a few other items of use, such as a knife and spoon, an old compass, and a couple names. All in all, he thought it was a great night. And they had spent time together as a family.

~~~

Alfred wasn't sure how he had been put on this detail, but now that he was here, he realized that it was a shit job. It sounded like something easy, folding towels and washcloths, but there were so fucking many of them, and more coming to him all the time, that he knew he'd be doing this fucking thing forever. Just as the next load, like hundreds of pounds of them, came to him, he realized that he was all alone in the big room.

He wasn't one to frighten easy. In fact, Alfred was the person that usually did the scaring. But here, alone in this room, all he could think about was every horror movie he'd ever seen about prison. There was no way he was going to be caught with his pants down. Not ever. And when he heard the door shutting nearby, he felt his ass clench up so tightly that he wondered if even a fart could have gotten past it.

"Who's there?" He didn't answer the voice that sounded so far away. If he had to spend the night huddled up on these towels to avoid being raped, then so be it. "Anyone around? Hello?"

The man came around the corner just as he was looking for a place to hide. He was a guard, and Alfred let out a long breath. Safe. He felt like he'd just dodged a great deal of pain. When the guard asked him what he was doing, he was so relieved that he told him what he'd been thinking.

"I thought for sure you were here to rape me. I don't

swing that way, and I would've put up a fight. You have no idea how relieved I am that it was you and not an inmate." The man just stared at him. "I don't suppose you could get me off this detail, could you? I mean, I'm not stupid or anything and could use a job that didn't have me standing on my feet all day. Maybe something cushy?"

"We don't allow that sexual stuff around here, though I'm sure that it happens, but we don't allow it." Alfred told him he was glad for that. "There aren't any jobs around here that are cushy. You're in prison, and from what I've heard, for a long time too. So you might as well not even ask about them. By the way, why didn't you go out when the rest of them did? At the end of the shift?"

"I didn't hear anyone leave. I've been sorting this mess. There are a great many towels, don't you think? I mean, how long is this for, a week or two?" He told him it was daily. "There are this many towels washed every day? Christ, that's a shit load of laundry."

"Don't curse." He nodded, wondering where the prison system picked these guys up. "I don't like a dirty mouth. You'll curb that right now, or I'll do it for you."

"Sure, sure. I can do that." He started folding the towels and wondered how many more he'd have to do before he was able to leave. "What time do they serve dinner around here?"

"Soon. You hungry?" Alfred told him he was. "Good. Lunch today is something fitting. It's one of my favorites."

It was creepy the way he said it, but Alfred was sure he was still in the mindset of being afraid. So, he moved a stack of the towels to the shelf where he'd been told and started on some more of them. After about ten minutes, the guard moved out of the room.

He'd never liked being alone. Even when he was at his office, he had the door opened to his front rooms so that he could see people coming and going. He might not have engaged with them, but knowing they were there helped. But here, he was beginning to think he might enjoy being in a room by himself. It was certainly safer, he thought.

Alfred was going to have to find him someone that could grease some palms for him. Menial labor wasn't his cup of tea. And he felt as if he'd been tricked into coming here. Like that fake lawyer. He should have checked his identification, but he'd been waiting on an attorney and had thought he'd arrived. Well, he'd know better the next time.

The noises of the washing machine stopped and the room was plunged into darkness. This time he didn't wait to find out who was there, but hid under the table he was working by. The legs of two men joined him, and he didn't move as they began doing the towels. He felt stupid for getting down there, and wondered how he was going to make an appearance without looking stupid. Just as he was just going to stand up and not mention it, the guard came back.

"You guys usually work in the dark?" No one said anything that Alfred could hear. "Ah, I see. You have to be in the dark. Vampires and all. Well, keep up the good work."

"You should have left the lights off." The guard asked why. "Because that way you'd not have to see what it is we're going to do to you. Killing you will be quick."

The scream was cut off when the men beside the table moved. Or he supposed they moved. As he stayed hidden under the table, blood began to pool at his feet. The guard was dropped then, and his dead eyes stared at him. Alfred knew he was dead; his throat had been ripped out, and the amount of blood had him thinking that every drop of him had spilled out. For vampires, he was surprised that they didn't drink it up instead of letting it fall to the floor.

Alfred didn't move. Didn't even take a deep breath while the two men continued to fold towels or whatever it was they were doing. Nothing was said between them, but he had a feeling that they were still communicating. Just as he thought he might get out of this, someone touched him from behind and he found himself being held high above the floor. His bladder let go just as the man holding him smiled.

Fangs. He knew that as vampires the man would have them, but these were sharp and long, like he'd taken a file to them to make them extra pointy. And when he looked into his eyes, he could see that they were as red as the blood that had been spilled. This man wasn't a regular vampire, this one was a killer.

"You're Alfred James, aren't you?" It didn't occur to him to lie. He wasn't even sure he could have spoken, so he just nodded. "We were sent to find you. To make you pay. Not that we'd charge her, but she did make it very worth our while to come here. You have some extremely powerful enemies, Alfred."

"I have money. A great deal of it. It's yours if you don't do this." The man shook his head and told him he had no use for money. "I don't want to die. I'll pay you twice as much as the other person did. Just let me go and I'll pretend none of this ever happened."

"Sadly, he is now dead. And I told you, we have no use for money. We want to kill you, especially after we heard what sort of person you are." They all three looked at the dead guard on the floor. "Everyone knows better than to trust a vampire. And why on earth would someone let us in to a feeding ground like this? It's not a smart thing to do."

"Who sent you?" The man holding him put him on the floor. "Tell me who contacted this person to have me killed. I deserve to know, don't you think?"

"Yes, you might deserve it, but that does not mean that we will tell you. This is the one person we do not what to cross. And as you are to be killed, we will do it." There was a tinkling sound, like laughter or bells. Then someone said to tell him. "It matters little now, I guess, but Flora sent us."

"Flora? I don't know a Flora. Is that her last name or first?" He said it was her only name. "That's not right. Everyone has two names. Who is she?"

The bug moved by his face quickly and he swatted at it. He didn't hit it, but when it landed on the shoulder of the man in front of him, he stared at it. It was a tiny person. With fucking wings.

"I am Flora." He nodded, mesmerized by her size and how beautiful she was. "You have caused too much trouble, human, and I wish you dead."

Cultured, it was all he could think about when she spoke. The French accent was lovely, and seemed to go well with her beauty. Then he realized what she had said and he let his anger go.

"Now, wait just a minute here. You can't be killing me. I'm here to serve my sentence. I don't know who you think you are, but you're not in charge of me. I don't deserve to be dead, as you call it." He didn't want to be here, but right now that was all he could think of. "Why would you care if I'm dead or not?"

"You hurt Sunny." He asked what she had to do with her.

"She is my friend, and her thoughts of you getting released are haunting her. I will take away her haunting by having you killed. It will work out well for her. Then she will be well for the new baby when it arrives. Stress will not help her."

"What about what she did to me? She ruined my business." Flora told him that he'd done that all on his own by being a bad man. "Bad man, huh? Why don't you let me show you what a bad man is? I could whip your ass in a second. Hell, sooner. If I win, then you let me go."

"Deal."

She agreed much too fast, but it was too late for him to ask her why she'd done that. Before he even saw her move, his body felt strangely light. Looking down at himself, he could see nothing different, but then he tried to look at her again. She, with the two men, were gone.

His left arm just fell away from him. He wasn't sure that was right, and reached down to pick it up. Blood was going everywhere, and he couldn't figure out how to get it to stop. Just as he was ready to call for help, Alfred fell from his legs.

He sat there, lying on his side. His legs had been cut off from his body at the hips, and he knew with certainty that he was going to bleed to death, slowly but surely.

Staring at his parts, he thought it slightly comical that his left leg was still upright while the right had fallen to the side. His arm was there too, looking as if it were holding it down. Blood was everywhere. The neat pile of towels he'd been folding had fallen over in it and were now soaking up the mess. Alfred felt himself get weaker and weaker.

"Hello." He looked at the person in front of him, not having a clue who it was. His mind was beginning to feel weird, and he only stared at the person. "I'm Tanner, friend of the Whitfields and to Sunny. I'm to wait until you are dead before I clean up. You should know better than to fuck with a fae. They're very callous, as well as excellent killers."

He thought of the little bug and closed his eyes. Alfred was going to die, there was no doubt about that, but a little bug had done it. Just as his mind was shutting down, along with everything else, he felt a punch to his chest and opened his eyes once more.

"I so love a good fresh heart. The blood is still warm."

And as he died, Alfred watched the man eat his heart.

Chapter 14

Josh sat on his unfinished porch and watched the sun going down. He hadn't gotten much done today, but felt like it had been enough. Blake joined him a few minutes later and shifted to himself. There were clothes in his car for each of them, and Blake dressed then sat beside him.

"I'm going to take you up on your offer." Josh nodded and took the bottle of beer that was handed to him and set it on the wood by him. "Adam said that he'd buy out my share of the ranch that we're running, and Mom and Dad are going to help him out when he needs it. I don't think he will, but you never know."

"No, you don't. What changed your mind?" Blake didn't talk much since Grandma had passed away. Even when he was asked a direct question, he'd only say the barest of words to convey himself. "I have three houses on the market right now that I won't be able to unload until spring. They're ugly as sin without the prettiness that flowers can bring to them."

"You think that I can do pretty? I don't, in case you care,

but I'll give it my best shot. And, I think that when offered again, I'm going to take Flora up on the fae for me. They know flowers and such better than anyone I know." Josh just looked at his brother. "I know the difference between a weed and a flower, but to make them look good in front of a house, I don't know if I can do that."

"You just have to know what would go good with the colors of the house. You know, like if the house is a plain brown, you'd know what colors would look good there, as well as if they're low maintenance. People really like low work in their yard. I hear that a great deal when showing a home." Blake nodded and set his own untouched beer on the floorboards between them. "You and me, we'll buy the nursery and then open it in the spring as our own. I'm not the realtor, so there won't be anyone questioning our interest in it, nor the fact that we're going into business for ourselves."

"So, we're going to do this? Go into business?" Josh told him they were, if he was willing. "Yes, I'm game. As I said to you before, I'm tired of farming and running a ranch. There are so few horses on it anymore anyway, so that's not even a big deal. I need a change."

They sat there for another hour, neither of them saying much, just enjoying the night. Josh invited his little brother to stay in the camper that he was using, and he of course turned him down.

He watched his brother move toward the yard. When he stopped, Josh was sure he was going to tell him that he'd changed his mind again, and needed to think on it some more. But he stood there for several seconds before he spoke.

"Those houses you have. Any of them all right to live in? I mean, that are empty and waiting for someone to simply move into?" He said they all were, just not marketable for their size. "Big or small?"

"Huge. Like bigger than Evan's house. I haven't had the right person come along yet. I will in the spring, but for now, they're just sitting. Why?" Blake nodded. "You interested in getting yourself a house? I'll even cut my commission out if you want one of them."

"No need for that. I can afford it." He started away again and turned back. "I want the biggest you have. Lots of bedrooms. I'd like to move in as soon as possible. Before winter sets in too deeply. I have things to move into a house… not a lot, but I've been thinking on that as well. Do you have one?"

"Yes, I have several that I can think of right now. But why do you want a big house?" He only shrugged. "You planning on adopting a bunch of kids, Blake? I have to warn you, they do ask a lot of questions. Just spend ten minutes with Evan's youngest boy, Elliott. I think he's going for some sort of record. And sometimes his questions are just repeated to you several times but in different ways. He's a cute kid, but damn, can he make you want to run."

Blake said nothing about the kids, but did ask how big a house he had. There were several that would suit the bill, but he was still curious about it. But knowing his brother, he'd not get a thing out of him until he was ready.

"There is a six bedroom that has three bathrooms. Not a good ratio. Also, I have an eight-bedroom house that has four baths. Doesn't seem as good, but it's one of those divided bathrooms, one for two bedrooms each. Then there is the biggest house. Eleven bedrooms, six full baths, and two half baths that can easily be converted into full if you need them. Full basement that's finished, with an outside walk and patio. Also, the master suite is on the main level of the house with its own deck and hot tub. It's a monster of a house. Lots of windows that have a spectacular view of the mountains behind it, and a six-car garage. Divorcee has decided to sell it so his wife can't have it." He told him the price. "Which includes sixty acres of the most beautiful land around here. It's the one that I would buy if I was looking for a big house. And some of the work inside is something that a cook would love. You want to see it?"

"I'll take it." He nodded for some reason; Josh had known that he would. "Any furniture with it? I mean, a divorce case usually means stuff like that."

"Yes, it's full. I can find out the price on it if you want." Blake nodded then smiled. It was the first one he'd seen on his brother in a long while. "You going to tell me why you want a big house like this? You're not out to find yourself a mate, are you, Blake?"

"I'm going to see about taking on some kids, yes. As for a mate, I'll think on it. They're a lot of fun, I'm thinking. But who would want an old broken-down farmer like me? Even if I do help run a nursery, who in their right mind would want to try and train me?" Josh wasn't sure he was kidding until he laughed. "I'm not opposed to having a mate, but I do want children now. If she comes along, great. If not, then I'll have someone to comfort me in my golden years. You let me know about the house and furniture, and I'll meet you at the bank. I know I don't have to ask you, but if you could get me a good price, then that'll be wonderful too."

It was sad, perhaps the saddest thing he'd ever heard, and it bothered him on so many levels when he left. His brother was willing to find a mate but really didn't care. Not that Josh was going out to find his either, but Blake was a nice man. Josh sat on the deck, wondering, not for the first time, about his own mate.

What sort of person would she be? Sweet and kind? Or someone that had a past that would come with her? He supposed everyone had a past, but he didn't want to have to kill someone right off the bat for her. He wondered what she'd be. Human? Another tiger? Not that it mattered, he supposed, but it would be kind of fun to figure out.

Dylan could run a country, he thought. She was that good. And kick ass while she was at it. She had the ear of the president, met with him weekly, and did things that he, as a tiger, would never do.

Sunny was...well, Sunny was just as badassed. She was smart. Very good at getting to the meat of a problem, but she was also soft and gentle. He supposed that she could tear into a man without any trouble too, but she would be slicker about it, not straight on like Dylan.

Josh loved his family. Mostly he loved that they were there when they needed each other. He walked to the camper his parents had used a great deal when they'd all been younger; they had loaned it to him, just until his house was finished.

It was still in excellent shape for being slightly outdated. They had kept it in the barn for the most part, and had it worked on every spring, even though they might not use it. Going inside, he made an offer on the greenhouse for him and his brother. Then he put in a bid for the big house for Blake and went to bed. Tomorrow they were going to put the siding on his house, and he was helping them out as much as he could. As he lay there, he thought of his conversation with

Blake again.

Would he find a mate? That question had come to him more and more over the last few weeks since two of his brothers had found theirs. Josh wasn't opposed to finding her. He was actually looking forward to having someone in his life that was there for him and him for her. But he was also afraid.

He knew little about women. He dated, of course, and had a good time around them. However, they were a mystery, as he supposed they were for every man. Even his brothers who had mates. But they were, for the most part, out for as much fun as he was.

There was nothing permanent about their relationships. And so far as he could remember, he'd never had a woman stick around for more than a couple of dates before they moved on, or he did. And always on good terms. It was fun, but he was ready to settle down, he supposed.

But being personal beyond sex, he didn't have a clue. Was he a romantic? He used to think of himself as one, but now, he had been watching his brothers with their mates, and he realized that he wasn't. Did he treat women, any of them, with respect? Yes. His mom would have killed him by now otherwise. But being with them daily...he wasn't sure what he had to do to make a woman want to be with him, especially his mate.

He supposed he'd have to cross that bridge when he got to it. Josh just hoped that he didn't mess things up too badly and have a woman, his mate, want to murder him from the get-go. It had made for some funny times with Evan, but he didn't want to be the butt of their jokes. His brothers could be cruel.

The next morning, he was on the ladder when he saw the men walking across his property. He didn't like the way that they seemed to be looking around every tree and under all the rocks. Not really, but Josh watched them carefully after warning the pack, which was nearby, that there were strangers on the land.

We've been following for the last mile or so. I don't know what they want, but they're sure curious about something. Twice now we've had to hide out when they pulled out some binoculars. Josh told them to be careful and that he'd let them know what they were after. *I appreciate it. My dad is here too. He is the one that alerted us to them.*

Josh got down off his ladder but didn't approach the men. Two of his brothers were there, and he was glad when they came to stand with him. The larger of the two men, weighing in at about three fifty, put out his hand as soon as he was near enough to touch him. Josh and his brothers ignored it.

"My name is Ethan Haynes. You the owner of this house?" Josh asked him, instead of answering, why he was there. "Oh. We're out looking for someplace to put in a development. Housing. Just out scouting the land, so to speak, and finding if there is a lot of it to sell. I hadn't realized that this had gone on the market. You being a realtor and all, I guess you'd have an inside to that sort of deal. Am I right?"

"No." Adrian and Blake moved away from him, but not too far. They were watching the other man, who was armed, he'd just noticed. "This is private property. I'd very much like for you to get out of here."

"Not very sociable, are you? Well, like I said, we're looking for land to buy up. And if you're willing to sell this, we'd give you a good deal on it. Enough that you could build elsewhere, should you like to sell." The card that was in the man's hand stayed there. "I tell you, I never met a more unsociable man before."

"So you said, twice now. And this is the second time I've asked you to leave here. I'm not selling." Haynes nodded, but didn't move. "Blake, can you call the police please? Tell them to bring out the wagon too."

"Wagon? Why would they need a wagon?" He explained. "Are you threatening to kill me, Mr. Whitfield?"

"Yes." The second man reached into his coat and Josh spoke again. "You pull that gun and you'll never eat with that hand again. Or anything else. Do you understand me?"

The low growl behind them had Haynes turning slowly. Josh had noticed the pack coming up, but apparently the two men hadn't. As Nate and the other wolves with him began to move closer, the two men backed up until they were almost touching him. They were an impressive lot, the wolves, and he was glad to see them.

"The police are on their way. They said to tell you that they were coming in when Nate called them." Josh nodded, but watched the men. "The sheriff asked that you not kill anyone before he gets here. He said the paperwork is burying him."

Josh didn't answer, but smiled instead. Haynes just stared at him. The sirens sounded a few seconds later, and that was when Haynes started talking. And he seemed to have a lot to say.

"I never meant any harm, young man. I'm just a man out looking for some property. You're the one that got all smart assed about it." Josh glanced at the man with him, then back at the bigger of the two of them. "I bet you're wondering why he's armed. He is because of the animals right behind us. There are a lot of wild animals around here."

"You have no idea." When the sheriff got out of his cruiser, he took Josh's hand in his for a hard, firm shake. It did not go unnoticed by Haynes. "This man and his partner are trespassing. I asked them, politely, twice, to leave, but they refused. And the younger of the two of them is armed. Itchy too…you know, jumpy, if you want my opinion."

"I tried to be nice, asking questions of the boy, but he was hostile and rude to me. I'm telling you right now, I did nothing wrong but be a nice person." Sherriff Brock looked at Josh then back at Haynes, who was smiling like he had not a care in the world. "We were out here surveying the area, and this pack of wild animals came here and started to threaten us. He's lucky that I don't press charges."

"Press charges about what? A pack of wolves chasing you off their land? Or this man, for protecting his own place? You're way off the beaten path, mister. And trespassing. As far as this man being rude to you, you're just lucky that they didn't bury you in the foundation here. We don't take kindly to people coming around and being an ass." Haynes sputtered a bit before Brock told one of his officers to help these men along. "They'll take you to your car and such. You just make sure that you head in the right direction, which would be out of my town. Otherwise, they'll never find you again, if you get my drift. Leave now and we won't pursue this any further. Stay, and I will not be responsible for what happens to you."

"This is no way to treat me. I'm planning on bringing businesses to this area. Homes and hotels. You're going to regret this."

He was put in the back of the cruiser and the other man was disarmed and put in another one. As they were taken away, Brock turned to Josh.

"What an idiot. He was asking all around town about property for sale. Something about he was here on a mission to make this town better. Nobody paid him any mind, but a couple of them called my office just before Nate did. Mrs. Cassidy came to my office to complain about them. Told me that they smashed up her garden when they were running from her dog. Poor woman. You think she'll ever figure out that it's a wolf protecting her and not her pup?"

"I hope not." They both had a good laugh, and Josh wondered aloud why they were there. "I mean, yeah, it's a nice piece of property, but there is a lot more of it outside of town. And cheaper too. He all but accused me of insider shit, about me getting this land illegally. When we all know that my parents have owned this land for as far back as their father's father owned it. I don't need this shit, Brock. It's hard enough selling houses around here without that crap going around."

"We'll keep an eye out for them now. He's staying at the hotel in Cambridge. I've got a few people looking into why he's here and who he might be working for." Josh thanked him. "No need. I was bored sitting in the office anyway. Oh, by the way, we'll all be there for the dedication today. Excited as hell about it too."

"We all are."

When Brock was gone, Josh decided he might as well get ready. If he was late to this thing, Dylan, then his mom, would kill him. The house was put on hold while the men working with him, including his brothers, got cleaned up. He was glad for this; it would be a nice touch to an otherwise shitty day.

~~~

Dylan thought things looked nice. She wasn't into foo-foo stuff, but she felt she'd done a bang-up job of making the little garden look inviting. Even the weather had turned nice and warm for the occasion. Evan wrapped his arms around her as their sons set up the chairs.

"Kyle is going to take pictures and Elliott is going to write up what happened here to add to them. Are you ready for this?" She nodded. "They're going to be here soon. The rest of the family is hiding in the house. She's either going to kill us all or fly away."

"I hope neither. And Henry sent her a nice dedication too. He had it printed up for her and put in a frame. She won't be able to carry it, of course, but we'll hang it where she can see it." Evan nodded and held her tighter while the boys were talking. "They're going to be all right, don't you think? I mean, I want them to be happy."

"They are. Elliott said that he enjoys having a meal and food when he wants it. And hot water. Kyle doesn't say much, mostly he just grunts, but I think that's a teenager's way of speaking. But he and my mom have hit it off well. He's been going over there after school every day to learn how to cook. She's teaching him the basics before she tackles things he wants to learn." She asked if he or his mom enjoyed cooking more. "I think it's about neck and neck right now."

Flora was to show up with Tanner. He knew, of course, what they were doing, but he'd promised not to tell her. He thought what they were doing was perfect for the little fae. All the rest of them could think of this was that it wasn't nearly enough for what she'd done for them.

191

When they showed up, Dylan asked Flora about the garden. "Some of the seeds have been in my bag for many decades. I wasn't sure there was still a heartbeat in them, but once they were in the ground, I could feel them coming to life." Dylan had noticed that there were small sprouts, and asked if they'd be all right with the coming cold. "Oh yes, my lady. The ground knows how precious they are, and told me that it would keep them warm."

"I'm so glad that you've taken over this garden." Flora said that she was working with Adam, not by herself. "But we want you to take it. For your own."

The plaque that had been made to stick in the ground was brought out, and the rest of the family followed. When Evan put the plaque in place, he pulled the plastic bag off and let her see it. Flora read each word out loud as they all stood there.

"To our dearest friend, Flora, a garden of her very own. Thank you for being a part of our family." It was signed simply, the Whitfields. When she turned to them, everyone clapped and thanked her. "This is too much, my lady."

"No, as far as we're concerned, there will never be enough to give you. You've given us our brother, friend, and family back. We can't ever properly thank you enough." Flora bowed and the rest of them did as well. Family, she knew, was very important to her, as much as it was to them. "Now we're going to have cake and drinks, and everyone is welcome to join us."

Dylan watched her sons. Something that she hadn't thought of herself as doing, much less feeling pride in having them around. Once she'd been hurt, she knew that there would never be any from her body. But Kyle and Elliott were perfect for them. They were a great addition to their growing family.

And they were growing by leaps and bounds. More children were set to come to them, she hoped. Sunny was going to have a baby in a few months. There were others too, not by blood, such as Tanner and Flora, but still family.

They enjoyed the evening. It had been fun, watching the little fae thank everyone and being told over and over it wasn't enough. She told them all that the garden would be wonderful come spring, and that she was looking forward to having them see it. That was another thing that Dylan liked, knowing that there was going to be a spring and another fall and summer. The future didn't seem so distant to her any longer. Nor impossible to imagine.

When the family left, she sat down at her computer to look up the men who had been on the property earlier. She had names...however, they weren't showing up as living. The man who had called himself Haynes had died back in the early nineties at the ripe old age of ninety-four. And the other man, Rooster Sharp, had died in the late nineteenth century at the age of twelve. Finding information on them had been easier than it had been to find out about the company they supposedly worked for.

"What sort of company do you suppose Walnut Industries would be? If there was one?" Evan asked her what she meant when he joined her in the office. "They left a calling card with Mrs. Cassidy that said Walnut Industries and nothing more. While the one that they'd dropped at Josh's house said Parker Real Estate. Which exists, but the company isn't sending out land surveyors at this time. And they have no desire to expand their search to anywhere near Ohio. So, that leaves us with a whole lot of bullshit."

"Then what do you think they were doing?" She said she had no idea, but she wasn't giving up. "I really didn't think you would. Before I forget to tell you, Brock said that the serial numbers for the gun were gone. Acid, he thought. Anyway, he's taken ballistics of it and will know more soon. I figured you'd want to do your own, so he's bringing the gun and ammo that he found on the guy over tomorrow. Nothing they can hold them on after they paid the fine for trespassing."

"He gave me the phone numbers they had on their phones too. Someone at the office is looking into those. This is getting more and more fucked up with each minute." He told her that he had to agree. "Did you see the look on Flora's face when we told her that she could plant anything she wanted around the house? I don't know much about décor and shit, but I have a feeling that we're going to be a showcase soon. Especially in the spring."

"She'll have a good time, we'll have a nice yard, and everything will be good. At least in that department." Evan stood up. "I'm going to bed. I was hoping you'd join me."

"I'd love that." They were walking hand in hand when her phone rang. Not the public one, but the one from her boss. "I have to take this."

"It's fine, honey. I've left you enough to run to the hospital." She nodded and smiled at him as she answered. "Hutch here. Got something for me?"

"The men are working for a little group called the Sheppards. A group funded by mostly rich people looking to shoot themselves a big game." Dylan told Evan what Henry told her. "There is some speculation that these guys go after more than big game. Humans for one. Another is each other. A lawsuit from about ten years ago was brought up against this group, but nothing ever came of it. I'm not sure if they settled or what, but you should be able to find that out. The picture of the older man brought up nothing so far. But the younger man, he's involved directly somehow. His name is Thomas Langley, goes mostly by Tommy. He has a reputation for being a hot shot of a negotiator. As in shoot first and walk away without consequences."

"So, we have a bunch of rich fucks messing in our part of the world and thinking to kill off a few of the people around here. I don't like it." Henry said he didn't either, but that was all he'd been able to unearth so far. "All right. With a name, I can look deeper. I have some contacts that can find out about the suit against them too. And perhaps why they think here is a good idea."

"Good luck." Thanking him, she put her phone away. Dylan looked at Evan as he stood there leaning against the railing to the second floor. She told him everything.

"Sounds like you at least have more than you did before. I mean, you have the name of one of them, and a business name. You've worked with less." She told him that she liked a challenge, but this was really skimpy. "I have all the faith in the world in you. If anyone can do it, love, it's you." She snorted at him. And he, of course, laughed at her.

As they made their way up to bed, she thought of something else. They'd been looking not just for land to have their little games on, but also game, she'd bet anything. She would have to warn Nate and his pack about them, as well as any other shifters on their land. This was going to cause so many problems if she didn't get it figured out, and soon.

David

Chapter 15

Rachel watched her sister as she made her way toward her. Carter didn't look like she did ten years ago, nor as if she cared either. As soon as she was close enough, she asked if she could hug her. Carter consented, but she didn't return it. It was going to take a long time for either of them to come to terms with this.

After loading her meager belongings in the trunk of the car, she got in. Carter moved too, but slower than her, watching every little thing around her, she supposed, waiting for someone to tell her it was a joke. It wasn't…her little sister was free.

"I set you up at my apartment." Carter told her that she had to go to the halfway house. "I know, but only for a month. Or until you find a job. Which won't be easy, not with the economy the way that it is."

"Nor with having spent so much time away from everyone and everything either." There was that, she thought, and decided that now was as good a time as any to talk about it. "I don't want to talk about it at all, Rachel. Just let it go."

"I know you don't, but we have to. You're going to be all right now. You've been cleared of everything, and you're free. I just wish I could have done something sooner." Carter told her that she'd tried. "I know that, but you should never have been caught up in this at all. Mom and Dad, they fucked you over badly."

Their parents had let their daughter go to prison for nine years for them. And no matter how many times Carter had told them that she'd had nothing to do with them, they dragged her down until it was evident to the higher ups that she had done just what they'd said. Set up the plan for the robbery, executed it, and then killed an officer of the law when she'd nearly been caught.

"Have they been located yet?" Rachel said that they'd not. "Figures. They were always very good at that. Disappearing just when things were ready to hit the fan. I'm guessing that now that I'm out, things will heat up for them."

"You'd think that, wouldn't you?" Carter asked her what she meant. "They're washing it under the rug. Probably because they fucked up by convicting a seventeen-year-old for a crime that she had nothing to do with. As you told them several hundred times."

Carter didn't say anything but looked out the window. She wanted to get through to her. Tell her that things would be all right now, but she also knew that her sister was hurting. Hurting in ways that simply being set free might not ever fix.

She'd been just that, a kid celebrating her seventeenth birthday, when the police had arrested her. The kids with her, all ones that Carter had broken ties with when she'd been arrested, were shocked, but didn't really see that the police were wrong. She and Carter had come from a bad family.

"I have to check into the home." She told her that she'd gotten permission to have lunch with her first. "I don't want to, Rachel. I'm not sure that I know how to act around regular people. And you know what it's like for me when someone touches me."

"I know, sweetie, but it'll just be me and you. No one will have any idea that you were just released." Carter said she would know. "I can take you there, but I really wanted to spend some time with you. Please?"

"All right." Rachel wanted to find her parents and kill them herself. "But don't expect me to eat all that much. Okay? No pushing."

"Right, I won't." She knew that. After having a visit with the prison doctor, she'd been told a lot more than Carter had ever told her. Like about the ability that she had. And from what he said, she'd always had.

"She is telekinetic, the art of telekinesis." Rachel had asked him what that meant. She had an idea, but didn't want to believe it. "She is quite good at moving things with her mind. Not only small objects either. I've seen her move a car. It's speculated that she's had this since birth, because of how good she is at it. Controlled, I guess you could call it."

"And what have you told her about this?" He paled a little, and it frightened her. "You've told someone that wants a piece of her, haven't you?"

"No, I can't." She waited for him to clarify for her, and when he did, she was even more afraid. "The car that she moved? I was in it. She told me that if I mention what she could do to anyone, she would kill me. I thought it an idle threat until she lifted my car up and swung it around several times before she sat me back on the ground. And she spoke to me through my radio. I have to tell you, Rachel, I think your sister has a great many things going on in her head that she hasn't told anyone. And she terrifies me."

"I won't hurt you." Rachel looked at her sister and asked her what she meant. "I know that he told you about me—it's why Mom and Dad hated me so much—but I'd never hurt you."

"I know that." She wondered briefly how much her parents knew about their daughter.

"They knew some. Not a lot, but enough that when they robbed the bank, they knew that getting me blamed for it would get them out of their hair. I thought I'd be safe in there."

"Carter, can you read my mind?" Her sister nodded to her when she stopped the car at the restaurant. "Why didn't you tell me? Why didn't you at least let me know?"

"You not knowing saved your life." She got out of the car and Rachel sat there. Saved her life? She wondered what that had meant, but followed her into the restaurant. After they ordered and were awaiting their food, Rachel tried to think how to ask her sister what she'd meant when she started talking.

"Just before I was arrested, Mom came into my room and saw something. It wasn't much, just a book coming to me, but she freaked out. When she asked me what the fuck I was doing, I explained to her that she'd seen nothing. That she was dreaming." Rachel nodded, but said nothing. "She brought Dad in then, and they beat me until I did it again. And again. And again. By the time I was finished proving to them that I was able to do it, they'd broken my arm and had beaten me with Dad's belt."

"I remember you being hurt." Carter nodded and waited for her to continue. When the implications of what had gone on hit her, she felt her belly churn up. "They told you that if you didn't do whatever it was they wanted, then they would come after me. They used me against you."

"Yes. You were gone, making it on your own. I didn't want them to fuck that up for you." Rachel wasn't sure what she could say to that. Their parents were sadistic fucks, and would have done just what they had threatened. "Being in prison, behind the wall of doing what they wanted, where they couldn't visit me, I was safe too."

"Then why now? Why did you suddenly decide to talk? You could have gotten out at any time. I could have seen you more often." Carter looked away, then back at her. "Tell me, Carter, please?"

Instead of answering her, Carter lifted her hand. It was a simple gesture, but one that made her fearful when a small flame appeared in her palm. And with that, it changed and morphed into different shapes that she could see were their parents.

"They're coming here. And when they do, things will not be easy for anyone." Rachel asked her what they wanted. "Me. They've sold me out. Told someone that wants what I can do."

"Is there more?" Carter nodded. "Should I be worried? Should they be worried? I don't want you hurt again, Carter. I don't care one fig for them, but I don't want you to be hurt or taken away."

"They should be worried more than anyone. May I touch you?" She told her yes. "So that you might see what I know? It won't hurt you, but you'll be able to see what I can pertaining to them. You should say no, but I think that it will save your life if you know."

"Show me." The touch was gentle, almost too gentle for her to realize that her sister had done what she'd asked. But before she could ask what now, she saw them.

Her parents were in a car, arguing. And when the sound was turned on, it seemed—unmuted—she also heard them. Rachel felt her body stiffen, her blood freeze.

"When we get there, you take care of Carter, I'll deal with Rachel. Rachel may get hurt over this, but it won't matter to us much once we have the money. You know what you're to do, don't you, Lee?" He told their mom that he had it. "Once we have Rachel where we want her, then Carter will do what we want. Damned kids ought to be glad we didn't smother them in their sleep a long time ago."

"You sure did try a few times. Wondering now if it was Carter saving Rachel all this time. Ever think of that?" The touch to her hand had her grabbing tightly. Her sister…she'd protected her a great deal. "That man, he said that he'd give us the rest of the money as soon as he had Carter. Then we'll have to deal with Rachel. She's not going to like this one bit."

"Then we'll take care that she doesn't matter. Lee, we deserve this. More than anyone. Having a freak in the family, it's made us look bad. And her getting out now, that's about the best timing we could have. It's an omen, I tell you. Someone is looking down on us." Dad laughed, and she left them just as Mom was speaking again. "I've always wanted to see if a body dropped from a tall building would explode like a melon. We should—"

Neither of them spoke but just sat there. The salads were brought and Carter played with hers. Rachel was no longer hungry. She needed to take a shower, scrub what she'd just seen from her. She looked at her sister again.

"When did they have this conversation?" She told her while she was watching them. "You can do that? Sort of zoom in on people without them knowing."

"Yes. And read their minds too." Rachel asked Carter if she could have killed them at any time. "Yes."

That was a great deal to think about. Too much really. When Carter said that she would like to go, Rachel didn't even bother with boxing up their salads to take with them. The outing, or whatever she had wanted, was ruined. But she had to have quiet, had to think. She wanted to talk more to her sister, but she didn't even know where to begin. Not even how to ask the million and one questions going through her mind.

As soon as she dropped Carter off, Rachel went home. She had a nice apartment, but the security sucked. She knew that in order to protect the two of them, they were going to have to do something more. Get some help from someone that did this sort of thing. Without thought to how she'd be able to repay her friend, she found her phone number and called. Leaving a message was difficult; she didn't want to say too much or too little, so she begged her to call.

"Hello, Hutch. You might not remember me, but I'm Rachel Compton. We went to school together. I know that you have some skills, a great many of them, and I'm in need of some help. My sister, Carter, and I are in trouble. Can you call me? Please? I'm pleading with you." She left her phone number. "It's my parents again. I hope you remember me."

Putting the phone down, she thought of what she'd seen, how she'd seen it. Carter was something powerful, and just a little scary. When she was getting ready for bed, she thought of Carter in prison all these years and how she had hidden away, much like she had but deep in a cell. Their parents were never going to let them go.

I love you, Rachel. Stilling when she heard Carter speak to her, she waited to see if she was dreaming. *No, not dreaming. But you can speak to me as well. I'm sorry that you had to find out this way.*

I'm sorry that you had to protect me so much. I'm glad that you did, but I'm sorry for it all the same. Carter laughed. *I called a friend of mine. She can help us, if in no other way than to tell me how to use a gun. From what I remember, she was very good at it.*

She can help you, yes. Rachel asked her if she could help her. *I don't need help, Rachel, I need peace. But I'm afraid that I won't get it.*

I'm so sorry. Carter said she was as well. *We'll get through this. Together. You have to trust me that I won't let them hurt you again. I'm going to get us safe.*

I'm sure that you think so, but we both know that they're not going to give up. It's not going to be as easy to make me do anything this time. I didn't rob that place. You believe me, don't you? She said that she did, but asked what she had done. *I sent you away.*

Long after they stopped talking, Rachel laid on her bed. Carter was powerful. With just what she knew she could do, people would want her. And that, no matter what she had to do, wasn't going to happen again. Rachel got up and started going over what she had…money, stocks, and anything else she could sell. Getting out of town was the only way she could help her sister. And she would too. No matter what.

~~~

Dylan sat behind her desk and looked at the computer screen. She had yet to call Rachel back, but she would, if for no other reason than to talk to her about what she'd been up to. But help her? She wasn't sure what she could do other than to have her parents murdered. But that wasn't an option, she'd been told.

"What if I just mussed them up a little? You know, put the fear of me in them." Evan said no again. "They're not good people. I don't know all the story here, but there can't be too much good coming from this. I need to call her and talk, but killing off the parents would help a great deal."

"No. You heard what Henry said. Something more is going on, and you need the facts first." She nodded and looked at the article again. "How did a seventeen-year-old get convicted of robbing someone when there were all kinds of witnesses to say otherwise? I mean, she didn't even put up much of a fight when they took her away."

"No, she didn't. And Rachel might not know either. But Carter, her name is, she's out now, in some halfway house to get her acclimated to the outside world again." Evan looked over her shoulder at the picture of the two of them. "When I knew her, she was having some issues with their parents. Not like the normal teenager versus parents sort of thing. But more like they'd leave them for days at a time, sometimes longer, so they could do things. I never knew if Rachel knew what that was, she never said. Then when they returned, she'd come to class beaten to shit and bloodied."

"What if we brought them here? I mean, for a few days anyway. It might get you more information than just talking on a phone." Dylan said that she wanted to go to them. "It's not far. We could make a trip of it."

205

"You can't go. You told me last night you have four surgeries over the next week. And I have no idea why, but I think I need to go now." He wasn't happy about being reminded of his work load. "Look, I'll take Sunny with me. She'll love the drive, and if anything hinky comes along, she can shift and eat them. I won't kill anyone unless I absolutely have to."

"You know, that is not as encouraging as you might think it is. But I can understand what you're telling me. All right, but you have to take someone else with you. One of my brothers." She was shaking her head before he finished. "Why not?"

"I'm going to take your grandda." Dylan laughed when he moaned. "He'll love it. Two women to talk to. And as you said, it's not that far of a drive. Just a couple of hours. We'll be there and back before you can miss me."

"I miss you already." Dylan told him to grow up. "I'm an adult, as you well know, and I love my wife. All right. I guess Grandda will be all right. But you have to promise me again, no killing of anyone unless you have to."

"I promise." She stood up and stretched. "I'm leaving as soon as I can gather the army. I don't know why, but I need to get to her now. I'll call her on the way."

"I wish I could go with you. But I trust you to be safe." She told him always. "Just come back to me in the same condition that you're leaving here in. Okay?"

"You take all the fun out of everything."

He laughed with her this time, and she made calls while he looked over the paperwork for his upcoming surgery in the morning. An hour later, they were packed up and on the road.

Whatever was going on, she wanted to get to the bottom

of it. And she would. Dylan had taken her extra guns and ammo for this thing too. She wanted to be prepared for all the things that could, and probably would, go wrong.

Before You Go...

HELP AN AUTHOR

write a review

THANK YOU!

Share your voice and help guide other readers to these wonderful books. Even if it's only a line or two your reviews help readers discover the author's books so they can continue creating stories that you'll love. Login to your favorite retailer and leave a review. Thank you.

AWARD WINNING, BESTSELLING AUTHOR

Kathi Barton, winner of the Pinnacle Book Achievement award as well as a best-selling author on Amazon and All Romance books, lives in Nashport, Ohio with her husband Paul. When not creating new worlds and romance, Kathi and her husband enjoy camping and going to auctions. She can also be seen at county fairs with her husband who is an artist and potter.

Her muse, a cross between Jimmy Stewart and Hugh Jackman, brings her stories to life for her readers in a way that has them coming back time and again for more. Her favorite genre is paranormal romance with a great deal of spice. You can visit Kathi online and drop her an email if you'd like. She loves hearing from her fans. aaronskiss@gmail.com.

Follow Kathi on her blog: http://kathisbartonauthor.blogspot.com/

www.ingramcontent.com/pod-product-compliance
Lightning Source LLC
Chambersburg PA
CBHW022101170626
46808CB00002B/533